DESTINED SOULS

ELLIE WADE

Copyright © 2022 by Ellie Wade
All rights reserved.

Visit my website at www.elliewade.com
Cover Designer: Letitia Hasser, RBA Designs
Editors: Kylie Ryan, Final Cut Editing and Jenny Sims, Editing4Indies

No part of this book may be reproduced or transmitted in any form or by any means, electronic or mechanical, including photocopying, recording, or by any information storage and retrieval system without the written permission of the author, except for the use of brief quotations in a book review.

This book is a work of fiction. Names, characters, places, and incidents either are products of the author's imagination or are used fictitiously. Any resemblance to actual persons, living or dead, events, or locales is entirely coincidental.
ISBN-13 ebook: 978-1-944495-32-9
Paperback: 978-1-944495-33-6

This book is dedicated to Karrie Oberg.
I'm so happy we've become friends in this crazy book world.
Thank you for all your love and support.
Readers like you keep me going.
Love you.

CHAPTER 1

CATERINA

How is it possible that my chest aches so much for a man I could barely tolerate? Let's be honest, I fell out of love with Stephen years ago. He's not a good person, let alone a decent husband. He's a pig and a jerk. He's cheated on me more times than I care to know. I was on the bottom of his priority list—a piece of arm candy, at best. I wasn't loved or respected. I wasn't cherished, and I deserve more.

Despite Stephen's qualities as a human, or lack thereof, I'm sad. Truly and deeply heartbroken. I'm mourning…what? I'm not sure. There's not much from my marriage to Stephen to miss, yet I feel a great loss.

Ten years ago, I was an eighteen-year-old supermodel in Prague swept off my feet by a confident, handsome, and romantic young entrepreneur. Stephen Harding was everything I'd ever wanted. He made me feel like a goddess. He pursued me with an undeniable passion that was impossible to ignore. When I gave myself to Stephen for the first time, I saw my future flash before my eyes in vivid color. Visions of love, laughter, children, and family—a lifetime of happiness—filled my soul, and I knew. He's the one—my one.

It was fate, and I was destined to be loved by this man. And yet—I wasn't...*loved*.

How could I have been so wrong?

I wanted my marriage to work. I tried to hold it for years after it was already dead. I knew it. He knew it. Everyone knew it. I'm certain I looked weak and stupid for staying so long. But, to me, marriage is meant to be a lifelong commitment, and I was determined to make it work.

My parents met when my mother was a teen, and they've been madly in love since. I thought when the blue-eyed man in his expensive tailored suit approached me at the after-party of a designer's show that it was the start of my happily ever after. I had found my soul mate young, just like my parents had. I was blissfully happy. Stephen whisked me back to America to start our life together, and I had no doubts it was just the beginning of my fairy tale.

It all happened so fast, but it didn't worry me because my parents' story had started in a similar fashion. Their relationship had progressed quickly, just as my relationship with Stephen had. They are the most in-love couple I've ever known. A relationship like theirs was my end goal, and I wanted it bad. I was certain that Stephen was it.

But I was duped. That charismatic man I fell for in Prague wasn't the man I married but simply one of his many personas—one he dropped as soon as the vows were spoken. Once I officially became his, everything changed. I ignored it for a while, making excuses—convincing myself that I didn't make a mistake. I was too stubborn to fail, yet that was exactly what was happening.

Perhaps, it's not Stephen I mourn or even my pride at having failed but the young girl full of hopeful fantasies about love and life. She came to the United States on Stephen's arm, sure that this was the start of the most amazing love story ever. She had no idea that she'd live some vastly different version, a sad and quite lonely alternative.

I no longer carry an immature idea of love, and I don't expect to find it again. I was hit with the hard reality, and it wasn't pretty.

Is there true love out there? Are soul mates real? Yes, I've seen it in my parents' and friends' relationships. But it's rare, and not everyone finds it. It's not for me, and that's okay. It has to be.

I'm enough. All on my own.

I am enough.

I don't need a man to validate me. I don't need an epic love to have a worthy life. Everyone's path is different, and mine is meant to be walked alone.

I suppose I mourn the idea of a happy marriage because mine definitely wasn't one. I hurt for something I wanted so bad but never had. I cry for the girl who believed a storybook ending was in her grasp. I'm consumed with guilt over the decade I wasted being away from my family to hold a man who wasn't worthy of the sacrifice. There's so much I wish were different, but I can't change the past. It's time to move on.

So today—I cry. Tomorrow is a new day that won't be wasted on the mistakes of my past. I'm leaving this life behind and going home to Moscow to be with my family.

"Is this seat taken?" A voice pulls me from my thoughts.

I lift my gaze from the martini sitting on the bar before me and turn my attention to the man at my side. "I'm sorry?"

"Are you waiting for anyone?" He eyes the empty seat to my side.

I shake my head. "Oh, no."

The guy is tall and fit. He has short disheveled blond hair and bright hazel eyes. His smile is warm, accented by a dimple on the right side. He seems nice and gives off a positive energy, but I don't want to be cheered up today. I'm in mourning.

I take a sip of the dry martini, and it burns my throat as I swallow. "I don't mean to be rude, but I'm not in the mood to talk to anyone right now," I say as he slides into the chair beside me.

Raising a hand, he orders two martinis from the bartender. "I get it, totally." He blows out a breath of air. "Shit day? I hear ya. You know I came here with my roommate? He's my best friend, cool dude and all but can be a little self-absorbed." He waves his hand before us. "A day at the MGM Casino—great bro date, right? We were gonna hang out, gamble, drink, and play some pool. Just something different from our normal parties. Then the guy gets all flirty with the blackjack dealer. Her shift ends, and he bails. He's God knows where doing God knows what with…Celia is her name."

The bartender sets down a martini in front of each of us. "Thanks, man," this guy says to the bartender before continuing. "Worst part is that he has the keys to the car in his pocket. So I'm stuck here an hour from home in a casino, day drinking by myself. Lame. Right?"

I don't say anything but take a sip of the drink he bought me.

"Oh man, your day is worse. Isn't it? Uh, I'm sorry." He drops his chin to his chest, rubbing the back of his neck. Something about his demeanor makes me trust him or, at the very least, want to. He has this air of genuine kindness to him.

"I just signed my divorce papers." I force a strained chuckle. "Here of all places. My ex was meeting with some clients in the restaurant in this building and gave me no choice but to come here to sign. I'm leaving the state tomorrow, and so as my final act as his wife, I had to drive to a casino to end my marriage. The papers have been ready for a while. It was just his last jab at me, making me work to leave him. I wouldn't expect anything less."

"I'm so sorry. I really am," he says, and his words seem sincere. He holds out a hand. "I'm–"

I cut him off. "Look, once again, not trying to be rude. You seem like a cool guy. It's just been a really shitty day or, if I'm honest, ten years of consecutive shitty days, and I'm not in the most pro-guy mood. I kinda want to be alone, and I definitely don't want to be hit on."

He releases a laugh. "Aw, man. Saying it like it is. Totally understand. Let me just say that I didn't get this awesome personality from having an easy life. This level of charm comes as the result of many years of struggle. I know what it feels like to be down and disappointed. In my humble opinion, it's always better to go through the hard times with a friend."

"I have wonderful friends, but it's just very personal and something I need to process on my own," I say.

"Riiight…or with a complete stranger who can be your friend for the day." I start to protest before he says, "Hear me out. No names. No truths. Just fun. Just today."

I turn to the side and quirk up a brow. He smiles wide, and his boy-next-door charm fills me with something resembling happiness, an out-of-place emotion on my melancholy day.

"It sounds weird, right?" he continues. "Just let it sink in for a minute. I mean, no one wants to be alone, especially on such an emotional day. I'm here by myself. You're here by yourself. Let's have fun, take your mind off your awful ex, and instead of being sad over something's end—celebrate new beginnings."

"With you?" I ask.

"Yeah." He shrugs. "No one better. We just have to go over the ground rules."

I bring the martini glass to my lips and empty its contents into my mouth. My head feels light and fuzzy. "What would those be?"

"Number one, we only speak in lies. Nothing based in reality. Today is about escaping. So I'll go first." He holds out his hand to shake mine. "Hi, my name is Bernard Peppercakes, and I'm an astronaut."

I can't help the giggle that erupts. It's out of place yet

feels so good. I shake his hand. "Hi, I'm Daisy Hotlips, and I'm a goat herder."

He gasps. "Really? Wow. I've always been so impressed with goat herders."

"Yeah, I mean…it's a difficult job."

"Well, I can tell you that being an astronaut is a piece of cake. Anyone could do it."

I nod. "You know, I always thought it was highly overrated."

"Definitely," he says. "So, Daisy, where are you from?"

"Bermuda," I answer.

"Oh, nice. I'm from Cleveland."

For some reason, I find his answer hysterical. "You couldn't come up with anything better than Cleveland? I'm disappointed, Bernard."

"I know, right? It just came to my mind first, I guess." A small grin graces his face, and I realize how adorable he really is. "Rule number two, this is a one-day-only adventure."

"Got it." I nod. "Won't be hard. I'm leaving for Bermuda tomorrow."

"Rule three is to have fun, get out of your comfort zone. And rule four is no mention of anything that makes you sad."

"Okay, I can get on board with all those. Any other rules?" I turn on the barstool so I'm facing him.

His gaze travels over my body, leaving my skin

tingling in its wake. "Just one, and it's more of a condition than a rule, per se," he answers.

"Okay, lay it on me."

"You have to promise you won't fall in love with me." His intense stare captures mine.

I swallow the emotion in my throat. "That's a promise I can keep."

CHAPTER 2

CAT

"You say that so easily without hesitation," Bernard quips.

I shrug. "Well, as I said, I'm just getting out of a horrible marriage, and I'm leaving the country tomorrow. So you're safe from anything resembling falling in love."

Bernard downs the rest of his martini. "I'm pretty sure you just broke rules one and four."

"What?" I gasp. "I did not."

"Are you sure about that?" He quirks a brow.

"No." I sigh. "You're right. So what's the penalty for breaking a rule?"

He bites on his bottom lip. His hazel eyes look off in

thought. "I got it. If rules are broken and called out, then it will be a classic dare situation. I'll give you a dare, and you'll have to do it."

"Oh, we'll see about that." I shake my head.

"Well, within reason."

I can't deny that the past half hour talking to this stranger has been the highlight of a very dark week. "Fine. Within reason."

Bernard waves his hands to get the bartender's attention and then asks for two car bombs. The bartender brings us two tall glasses of dark beer and two shot glasses of a creamy tan liquid.

"So your dare for breaking rules one and four is to do this Irish car bomb shot with me."

I scrunch my nose. "I'm not much of a shot person."

"Perfect, so this fits rule number three perfectly. Totally out of your comfort zone." He winks and scoots the tall beer toward me before handing me the shot glass. "So on my count, you're going to drop your shot, like the whole thing, glass and all, into the beer and chug."

"Chug that? That sounds awful."

Bernard laughs. "You'll be fine. You ready?"

Mirroring his motions, I lift my shot glass between my fingers and hold it over the large glass of stout.

"On the count of three. One. Two. Three," he says, letting the shot fall into his beer.

I follow suit and bring the tall glass to my lips and

chug. The taste is surprisingly good and sweet, but it's a lot of heavy liquid.

"Oh my gosh." I set the empty glass down on the bar and hold my stomach. "That was a lot. If I'm to be able to walk on this daytime adventure, I need to slow down before I pass out."

"Yeah, you are a tiny thing, so maybe drink some water before your next drink," he says with a grin.

"Good idea." I nod, my head fuzzy. "I don't think I'm a fan of dares. Let's go over the rules again."

He orders a bottle of Blue Moon beer for himself and a glass of water for me.

"Good idea. Number One: nothing but lies. Number Two: one day only. Number three: get out of your comfort zone and have fun. Number four: no mention of anything that makes you sad. And then, of course—the condition—which you said is a piece of cake."

"Yep, no falling in love. I can handle that one. The others, I'll have to work on. So what are we going to do on this day of fun?"

"Have you played roulette?" he asks.

I open my mouth to tell him no but remember the whole truth rule. "Yes, every day of my life since I was one month old. We had a giant roulette wall on my aunt Hilda's yacht."

"Nice." He chuckles. "It's a table, though. Come on." He extends his hand, and I take it.

"So how do you play it?" I ask as the two of us walk through the casino.

"Well, there are three octopuses…octopi? How do you say more than one octopus?"

I huff out a laugh. "Oh, my gosh. We need a truth pass or something because while avoiding real life is nice, sometimes I need to know the truth. Like how to actually play roulette."

"Yeah, you're right," Bernard says as we stop in front of a table with a wheel full of numbered sections in alternating black and red colors. A casino worker holds a white ball and drops it onto the spinning wheel, telling the people around the table to 'place their bets.'

"Okay, I got it," he says. "How about we each have a couple of phone-a-friend passes, and if said passes are declared, that will signify to the other that the truth should be spoken. But they'll have to be limited of course. Otherwise, what's the point of rule one?"

I nod. "That sounds good."

For some reason, Bernard is counting the buttons on his shirt. "Perfect," he says. "So we need a way to keep track, and it just so happens my shirt has eight buttons. Each time a phone a friend is used, I'll unbutton one button. When my shirt is wide open, free of all constriction, then we've used up all our truth cards. Sound good?"

I throw my head back and laugh, and it's so freeing. This guy is so perfect for me. It's true the universe didn't send me my true love in Stephen, but today, it sent me my perfect distraction.

"You realize this day is getting oddly complicated," I say, a genuine smile across my face.

"What is a day at the casino without some rules, conditions, and a handful of phone-a-friend options?" He grins, and it's both sexy and adorable all at once.

I smack him playfully on his arm. "I don't know, a *normal* day."

"Daisy, normal is overrated." He takes hold of his top button. "We're going to pretend this was done up in the first place. Okay?"

I nod.

"So you're cashing in a phone a friend?"

"Yes."

"Okay, so one button undone. Yes? Now, let me tell you about the game."

He proceeds to tell me about roulette and the different ways to play. I can place a bet on an individual number, odd or even, black or red, or rows called thirds. I'm rather tipsy, but I think I understand the concept.

"I got it," I say. "I want five on black, two on fourteen, two on six, and I'll do five on the second third," I call out to the lady manning the ball and wheel.

"Slow down there, Daisy girl. You must lay your money on the table, and the dealer will supply you with chips that you'll use to place your own bets."

"Oh, okay!" I say louder than intended.

Bernard lays a hundred-dollar bill on the table and tells the dealer that he'd like fifty chips for each of us. "What color do you you want?" He motions toward the stacks of chips.

"Pink, please!"

"Pink for the lady, and I'll take blue," he says.

A moment later, I have several stacks of chips before me. The dealer spins the wheels announcing to 'place our bets,' and I set to work on scattering my chips around the table. The ball lands on fourteen.

"I had fourteen!" I cheer, raising my arms in triumph. The dealer starts stacking chips onto the felt-lined table next to the chips I played on fourteen. I turn to Bernard, my eyes wide.

"Yeah, and you played even. So you win there, too. Great job." His face lights up.

The dealer pushes several large stacks of chips toward me. "Oh, my God! There's so many."

"Yeah, well, the numbers pay out thirty-five to one. So your two chips on fourteen made you seventy bucks. Then the odd and even pays out one to one, so your ten-dollar bet earned you ten dollars."

"So in one spin, I made eighty dollars?"

"Well, yeah, but you don't always get so lucky. So be careful with your bets."

I raise a brow. "You know, I believe you just told me a truth."

"I mean, knowing your payout is important, and part

of knowing the game." He pulls his bottom lip between his teeth, and the simple motion does something to my insides.

"Regardless, I didn't phone a friend, so you owe me a dare."

"Fair is fair," he quips. "Name it."

I pull in a breath. "Kiss me."

His eyes go wide. "Wait, what? Are you sure? You're kind of in a vulnerable place right now, and I'm pretty sure you're drunk.'"

"True and true but also irrelevant. Today is about escaping, right? Well, I want you to kiss me. And in the vein of going through the day in lies and not focusing on reality, I think we should also pretend we're newlyweds, and we've chosen MGM Casino as our honeymoon destination because we're that cool." I place my hands on his knees and lean in until our lips are a breath apart. The roulette table, the people sitting around it, and the chatter and beeps of the casino fade away as soon as his lips meet mine.

The kiss is slow at first. Yet even in their hesitancy, his full lips cause a warmth to heat my skin that I haven't felt in so long. This is the first *first kiss* I've had in over ten years, and in reality, the fourth one of my life. My body trembles as his tongue peeks through my lips, requesting entrance. I open my mouth, circling my tongue with his. My hands shake against his thighs as his tongue dances with mine. I know this isn't real and will all end tonight. I'm a broken Cinderella in this odd Alice in Wonderland universe where nothing makes sense. Even so, this kiss awakens a part of me that I'd long forgotten, and it hurts so good.

He pulls away and gasps. "Daisy." He lifts his thumb to wipe the tears from my cheeks. "What's wrong?"

"Nothing," I say truthfully. "That was great."

"Great kisses don't usually make women cry." He scoffs, wiping my other cheek.

"I haven't been kissed in years," I admit. I don't remember the last time Stephen really kissed me. But his kisses stopped well before the sex did, and the last time I slept with Stephen was three years ago. "I guess I forgot how good it felt." My words are vulnerable, but they're the truth, and it's freeing to speak them.

He leans in and presses his lips to mine in a chaste kiss. "I think you owe me a dare," he whispers against my mouth.

"I guess I do." I kiss him again.

He sits back and tells the dealer we'd like to cash out. Apparently, we cash in our colored chips for ones we turn into the casino cashier for money. It's all a little confusing. The dealer looks relieved as we collect our money chips and stand to leave. "Sorry, we can't help it," Bernard says to the dealer with a shrug. "We're on our honeymoon."

He grabs our chips and plants another kiss on my lips before we hurry away from the roulette table.

"Oh my gosh, she hated us." I giggle.

"Probably, but who cares." Bernard pulls me against him and kisses me again. Our tongues swirl, and my entire body heats, melting against him. This guy is an amazing kisser.

My arms are draped over his shoulders as I pull his face closer to mine. He's tall, hovering over me even with my high heels. He has to be at least six foot four, which is nice. Stephen was only an inch taller than me at five-eleven, which made him shorter than me when I wore heels…which was always, not that it really mattered to me. Yet having this man's strong arms wrapped around me and my body leaning against his as his mouth works magic is something pretty amazing. I'm soaking it all in, even if it's just for a day.

He leans back. "Now that we're married, it will be hard to keep my mouth off yours."

"I know the feeling." I cup his cheek. "So what's my dare?"

"Well, I'm taking you shopping."

"What? I love shopping," I squeal.

Bernard puckers his lips, a mischievous smirk on his face. "Yeah, but this will be a little different than you're used to."

CHAPTER 3

CAT

"This can't be your idea of shopping." I look around the gift shop. Everything in here has one of the Detroit sports teams' logos or the casino's logo on it. Everything. "This is all junk."

Bernard laughs. "Well, even though you look unreal, like incredibly fucking hot, in that tight dress and heels. That outfit looks uncomfortable. That dress is meant for a supermodel walking on the runway."

"A supermodel?" I scoff. "Can you imagine?"

"Well, yes, because you could totally be a supermodel. You look just like one. But today's about having fun, and part of having fun is being comfortable. So I'm getting you new attire for the day."

"In here?" I shriek.

"Yeah." He chuckles.

"But I always wear dresses and heels. I'm comfortable, I swear." He eyes my pointy-toed heels and quirks an eyebrow. "Listen, I stopped feeling my toes years ago. These don't bother me at all."

"Nonetheless, we're doing this."

"Fine. A dare is a dare, but I insist on paying. You already put down a hundred for us at the roulette table, and I don't want you to spend so much money on me."

"It's not a big deal," he says.

"Well, it is to me," I tell him. "I don't know what your money situation is, but I have plenty of my own, and I don't feel right taking yours. Please let me pay for myself."

Bernard stands looking over a shelf of Detroit Piston gear. "Okay, I'll agree to that, but you need to be careful. You're slipping in an awful lot of statements of truth."

"That could've been a lie. I mean, you don't know… nor are you aware that I know absolutely nothing about the NBA, so maybe a Piston's T-shirt isn't my thing."

He shakes his head with a tilt of his lips. "Why do I have a feeling that's a truth, too?"

I look at him pleadingly.

"Fine, since we're still amid this dare, I'll ignore your last two truth statements." He hands me a gray T-shirt. "Hold this."

I stare at the garment in disgust. Even my pajamas

have more style than this generic basketball T-shirt. "Alleged," I say.

"What?"

"Alleged lies because as we've gone over. You don't know."

He grins and pulls me toward him, his mouth capturing mine in a sweet kiss. "Why did I marry such a smart-mouth?"

"Because you've had a thing for goat herders from a young age," I say.

He chuckles. "True. Okay, let's see what else we can find here."

I follow him around the small store as he *shops*, if this can even be called that. With each new item he hands to me, my grimace grows. My buzz from the car bomb and two martinis seems to be wearing off, replaced by the horrible *fashion* I hold in my grasp.

"Turn that frown upside down," Bernard says with a chuckle. "You'll be fine."

When he's happy with his selection and I've paid, I make my way to the restroom to change. *Live a little, Cat.* I give myself an internal pep talk. When I step out of the bathroom stall, a stranger is staring back at me in the full-length bathroom mirror, one with horrible taste in clothing, nonetheless.

I'm sporting a gray basketball T-shirt, orange Detroit Tiger's—our professional baseball team—sweatpants, and a blue Lion's—our NFL team—ball cap. The gift shop didn't have shoes, so Bernard insisted on these furry MGM Grand Casino slippers. Detroit pride just vomited all over me, and it's not flattering.

A woman comes out of the stall beside me and eyes me from top to bottom. She gives me a strained smile and washes her hands quickly before leaving. I'm certain she thinks I'm insane.

The truth is, maybe I am. I'm galivanting around this casino, half-drunk, and making out with a complete stranger while playing the most complicated game ever. Yet this has been one of the best days I've had in a while, divorce included. So let people think what they want. I'll never see any of them again anyway.

Dropping my dress and heels into the gift shop bag, I take hold of the handles and head out of the bathroom.

Bernard starts clapping the second I step out into the lobby. "Oh, my God, yes! There's my hot wife."

Wrapping my arms around his neck, I pull his face toward mine, my lips eager to feel his. "My husband sure has a weird definition of hot."

"Are you kidding, Daisy baby? You'd be the hottest woman in this entire place—hell, this entire city—even if you wore nothing but a garbage bag. I have a feeling you're the most beautiful woman in any room you enter. Today is no exception. Any man would be lucky to have you and an idiot to let you go."

"Lies." I swallow. "All lies."

He pulls me in close and kisses my forehead. "You

know, all my life, I've been searching for a goat herder with amazing Detroit team fashion sense to be my wife. I feel like I was destined to find you."

"Maybe you were, Bernie. Let's go get some drinks, and then you can teach me another game."

"You got it." Bernard threads his fingers through mine and leads us to the bar.

We order drinks and some appetizers and talk at the bar for hours. Each of his stories is more ridiculous than the last, and I love it. My sides ache from laughter, and the sadness of my morning has been long forgotten. None of this is real, not even our names, but it's truly amazing at the same time. This man has managed to turn one of the saddest days of my life into one of the happiest. He's my angel for the day, and though nothing but falsehoods have left my lips, I feel like he knows me better than my ex-husband ever did. That thought is strange but somehow true.

We make our way around the casino playing the games, winning some and then losing right after. I've always thought gambling was such a waste, but I'm thankful for the distraction today.

"So the cherries are the best." I insert a twenty-dollar bill into a slot machine and hit the flashing button.

"Yes, and you want it to land on three cherries all the way across." Bernard sits behind me on the stool. His muscular thighs cage me in as his arms wrap around my middle.

He pulls my hair to the side as he places soft kisses down my neck.

"Does the machine ever let me land on the cherries, though?" The machine's wheels land on three different pieces of fruit, none of which are cherries. I look at the bottom corner of the screen to see how that combination gave me no money.

"Sometimes but not often. Bottom line is the casino usually wins. If casinos didn't make money, they wouldn't exist. You know?" His finger slides under my T-shirt and draws soft lines across my belly. I lean my head back against his chest.

"Then why do people continue to play knowing they'll lose money?" My voice is a heated whisper.

His lips tug on my earlobe. "The thrill of the chase, I guess. They play for a chance."

"I love being married to you." I smack the yellow button again, not even opening my eyes to watch where the pieces of fruit land. I couldn't care less about cherries or money. Instead, I concentrate on Bernard's lips, his touch, his breaths. The combination is intoxicating. I guess I understand gambling. Because hasn't that been what I've been doing all day with the man behind me? Clinging to the thrill of the chase, the chance that something good will come from this day.

It already has.

We've had an entire day of fun, laughter, and foreplay. Once I declared the honeymoon backdrop of our little game, neither of us has been holding back. It feels so real that I almost believe it.

"I love being married to you, too." His warm breath causes goose bumps to form on my neck.

I twist on the stool to face him and wrap my legs around him—a positive attribute to sweatpants versus a tight dress, I suppose.

"I've had the best day," I tell him honestly.

"Me too," he replies. He looks down at his chest, where only two buttons remain. "I need to use my last two phone a friend.

"Okay." I nod.

He reaches between us and unbuttons the second to last button. "First, are you a hundred percent sure that you have to move to Bermuda tomorrow?"

My heart clenches at the thought. The sliver of my brain that's not intoxicated comes through and reminds me that I'm just getting out of a ten-year marriage, and I've all but aged out of the supermodel life. I must figure out who I am and what I want with my life. Those questions require me to get away from everything I've known for the past decade. Going home to Moscow, to my family, is the only option. I know it in my heart.

"I'm sorry. I do. I have to leave tomorrow. I've already shipped all the important stuff back home. I have a suitcase upstairs in a room. I figured I'd stay here tonight since I fly out of Detroit in the morning. Today has been incredible, but it doesn't change my reality."

"I respect that. Maybe that's all we were supposed to be is one fun day."

"The best day." I grin.

He undoes his last button. "So for my last phone a friend, and I need the absolute truth from you, okay?"

"Okay." I agree.

"Do you want to move this to your room and celebrate our marriage the right way?" His tongue peeks out, licking his lips before he chews on the bottom one. It's almost more than I can handle. This man is so gorgeous.

"Yes, definitely."

"You sure. You know what I mean?"

"Oh, I know exactly what you mean."

"And you're positive?"

"Bernie, I've been imagining what you'd feel like inside me since the moment your lips touched mine at the roulette table. I'm absolutely positive. Plus, with your shirt wide open, you're halfway ready." I splay my hands across his chest.

"Venture a little lower, baby, and you'll see that I'm more than halfway."

He backs off the stool and takes my hand. I snatch up my purse and gift shop bag with my free hand while we speed walk out of the casino, leaving the beeping machines behind.

CHAPTER 4

CAT

Bernard's lips are on mine the entire way through the casino

"I've never done anything like this in my life." I pant as he pushes me back against the corner of the elevator. His hand slides up my T-shirt and beneath my bra.

He plays with my nipple as his lips continue to worship my neck, and I lose control of the noises coming from my mouth. I've lost it—all inhibitions, restraint, self-respect—and I don't even care. He could take me in this elevator, and I wouldn't object.

I've never felt so uninhibited, wanted, and free.

The elevator dings, and the doors open to my floor. We stumble out, and somehow, I manage to get my key card out of my purse and the door open. As it closes behind us, everything intensifies.

Our kisses are now frantic, our sounds animalistic. We make quick work of removing our clothing until we stand bare.

"You are the most beautiful fucking woman I've ever seen." He kisses down my body. "I can't even believe you're real." His fingers grasp my waist, pushing me back toward the bed.

When the mattress hits the back of my knees, I fall back. He drops to the floor at the edge of the bed and spreads me open. "I've been dreaming about this all day." He groans before his mouth circles the sensitive bundle of nerves between my legs. I cry out, tugging at his hair as he starts to lick me at the perfect speed. My body turns to mush as he works his magic. I've never felt anything like this. Never. Stephen ventured below only a few times in the early years of our marriage but never like this.

This man is making love to me with his mouth, and he likes it. It's not a chore for him like I always felt it was with Stephen. The passion in which his mouth moves, the groans vibrating against me, and his hand reaching up to massage my breast is incredible. A long-forgotten sensation starts tingling my scalp and starts to course through my body, lighting all my nerves on fire. My thighs start shaking, and I tug on his hair, needing something to ground me as I fall. The orgasm consumes me, and I'm a quivering mess of sensations screaming into the lust-filled space.

"Oh, my God." I sigh on an exhale as Bernard kisses up my body.

When he hovers over me, I reach my hands up to cup his strong jaw. "That was amazing." My words are soaked in emotion. Truthfully, it's oddly unsettling to feel so satisfied after years of famine and forever feeling as if I wasn't enough for the man I'd chosen to dedicate my life to.

Until this moment, I never realized how much of myself I hid away, how small I'd become. It's heartbreaking and liberating all at once. I no longer have to exist in the shadows of my marriage. I can boldly live life. I'm free.

"Hey." Bernard wipes an errant tear. "I hope that's a good tear."

"Oh, it's definitely a happy tear, a that was beyond incredible tear." I chuckle. "I'm sorry. I'm such a lame one-night stand. This isn't what you signed up for."

He lowers his face and kisses my neck. I stretch to the side with a sigh, allowing him access. "No," he says against my skin. "This is way better. You are a fucking goddess, and I'll never forget this day." He rests his elbows on each side of my face, caging me within his strength. His hazels hold my stare. "You want to keep going?"

"Of course." I thread my fingers through his short

hair and pull his face toward mine. "I don't remember the last time I wanted something more," I say against his lips.

He moans against my mouth and kisses me—soft at first before gradually growing in intensity. His lips are so familiar, a perfect match to my own. Our mouths move together, and our tongues dance as if they've done this a hundred times before. Everything about him comforts me. He's my haven, if only for today.

He pushes off the bed and stands. A shiver of loss runs through me. "What are you doing?"

The corner of his mouth tilts up into the most adorable smirk. "Okay, don't judge me. But..." He reaches for his discarded pants on the floor. "I thought this night might progress to here, so I stopped by the condom machine in the men's bathroom a couple of hours ago, just in case." He slides his hand into the pocket of his jeans and pulls out a few crinkly plastic squares. "I want you to know when I first saw you, looking so lonely and sad at the bar this morning, I didn't plan on this. I really just wanted to have fun and cheer you up."

"I know." I smile back. "I'm glad you came prepared, though. That's good." He fans out the condoms in his grasp. "Three? That's a little overzealous, don't you think?" I raise a brow.

He drops two of the condoms on the bedside table and opens the third. Pulling his bottom lip into his mouth, he stares at me lying naked on the bed. He rolls the condom down his long length, and my breath picks up speed at the sight.

"I don't know," he says through labored breaths. "With the way things are going, I'm afraid three won't be enough. If we only have tonight, we'll make it count."

All I can do is nod, wide-eyed, as he lowers to the bed and crawls over my body.

He positions himself at my entrance. "You sure?"

I lower my chin in agreement.

"I'm going need you to say it, Daisy baby."

"Yes, please," I beg.

He pushes into me, and we release a collective groan. Nothing has ever felt so good.

Circling my hands around his back, I pull him toward me. He kisses me, moaning into my mouth as he pounds in and out below. Just like everything else with us, the sex, too, is perfect. Our chemistry is off the charts.

Pulling his mouth from mine, he throws his head back in a moan. A sheen of sweat covers his muscles as he pumps harder. He's so incredibly sexy.

With each thrust, he hits a spot within me that causes me to see colors beneath my eyelids. The space around us is a collection of sounds—skin slapping, labored breaths, heady groans. It's intoxicating.

I gasp with the sudden build of another release. "Oh, my God, right there. Oh, right there…" I cry, clinging onto his biceps. I've never orgasmed during sex, and the crescendo toward release is complete ecstasy. "Bernie…" My voice shakes with the onslaught of new sensations. At this moment, I wish I knew his real name and identity because the man making me feel this good deserves to be truly seen.

A guttural scream explodes from me as the orgasm hits. My entire body quakes as he thrusts into me harder until he's groaning out his release.

"Fuck, fuck, fuck…" He shakes as he empties inside me.

He falls atop me, our sated bodies boneless and sweaty.

After a while, he rolls off me and entwines his fingers through mine, squeezing my hand. "I'm not letting you leave. I'm going to tie you up where you'll be my sex goddess forever."

I chuckle, releasing his grasp. I roll over and rest my cheek on his chest. "That was another first for me." I trace light circles over his abdomen.

"What was?"

"Orgasming during sex. I've always needed some sort of external manipulation, usually with my own hand. So that was… that was powerful."

"Oh, my God, I can't even…" he groans. "Every time you reveal something about your marriage, it makes me so mad. You deserve so much better."

"I know, and I'm going to get it."

"What else haven't you tried that you want to?" he asks.

"Different positions, maybe."

"Oh, that's a piece of cake. Anything else?"

I circle my mouth around his nipple, feeling it harden against my tongue. His skin tastes salty, and I desperately crave him. "I've never done it more than once in a night, so we could use up those other two condoms."

He trails his fingers down my spine until he's palming my butt cheek. "Well, that's a given."

As soon as the used condom is discarded and a new one put on, I'm sinking down on him.

I gasp, and Bernard smiles. He grabs my hips and starts moving me up and down atop him. "That's a whole new sensation, right?" he grits through clenched teeth.

"Yeah." My voice trembles. Riding him like this verges on painful because it's so intense. He's big and hits a spot deep within me that makes me cry out with each thrust.

"That's it," he coaxes me on as I pick up speed. My face scrunches, and I whimper with each deep penetration. "So good, baby," He pinches my nipples. "The climb is brutal, but I promise you the fall will blow your mind."

My release builds, and my mind warns me to stop. It's too much. Too good. My thighs burn as I bounce. A pained cry escapes each time he hits me deep inside. My orgasm comes hard and fast. I fall against him, moaning against his chest. I'm vaguely aware of him taking hold of my thighs and moving me over his length as he comes with me.

The night is spent talking, laughing, and kissing until my mouth aches. We use the third condom, and when we're done, I can barely keep my eyes open.

Bernard lies behind me, my back to his front. He pulls me against him, kissing my shoulder. His hand is splayed against my belly. It should feel weird spooning naked with a man I just met today, but it doesn't.

"Do you really have to go to Bermuda tomorrow?" he repeats his question from earlier.

"I do." I sigh. "However, I want you to know that this was the best day I've had in a long time, if ever."

"Same." He kisses the back of my head.

My eyes are closed. The darkness of slumber pulls me down as he whispers, "I'm going to miss you."

I'm going to miss you, too… I think as sleep finds me.

CHAPTER 5

CAT

Sunlight peeks through the window, and I start to wake. The first thing I feel is tired, but not the normal type of exhaustion. My body and muscles are heavy and sore. Memories from yesterday penetrate my foggy brain, and I reach back to feel him.

Only he's gone.

I sit up, my head dizzy. "Bernard?" I call out, my voice groggy.

There's no answer.

I look at the floor where his clothing no longer resides, and my chest aches. Sadness sinks into the pit of my stomach.

I shake my head and pull in a breath. There's nothing

to be sad about. He was never going to stay, and I made that clear. I can't be mad that he followed the parameters I set up. I'm leaving today, and that's what I should focus on.

Scanning the room, I search for my purse when a piece of paper on the desk catches my attention.

I jump up and dart across the room. A smile comes to my face when I see his writing.

My Daisy,

Careful not to break rule number two, *I left before daybreak. One day only.*

I wanted to stay, but I promised you one great day, and I hope I delivered.
It was perfect to me, something I'll never forget.
For you are incredible.
Bermuda is lucky to have you.
I hope you find everything you're looking for and more.
Be happy.
I'll never forget you.

Your Bernard

. . .

Tears course down my cheeks as I read the note over and over. I can't be sad over something I never had. Yesterday was a fantasy designed by a really nice guy. He wanted to cheer me up, and so he did. It wasn't real, though. Daisy Hotlips and Bernard Peppercakes aren't based in reality, no matter how real they felt.

I fold the note and slide it into the side pocket of my purse before heading into the bathroom to shower. I push thoughts of yesterday out of my mind and think about the fact that I'll be with my family again in less than twenty-four hours. I've missed my parents so much. We talk all the time and video chat, yet it's not the same. When I see them, I'm going to hug them tight and never let go.

Staring at my reflection in the mirror, I can't help but think of what Bernard would think. The form-fitting pants and flowy blouse cost around five hundred dollars, and that's not including my glorious heels with the famous red soles.

"Hey, at least I'm wearing pants on the plane," I say aloud. "It could be a dress, you know?"

My gaze finds the horribly ugly Detroit-themed pieces on the floor, and I pick them up. Folding them nicely, I place them in my suitcase. I doubt I'll wear them again, but I can't leave them behind. I hug the fuzzy casino slippers to my chest before setting them alongside the clothes.

As I'm zipping up my suitcase, there's a knock on the

door. My heart accelerates, and I rush toward it. *Did he come back?* I swing it open to find my best friend, Alma, and our mutual friend Quinn.

"Oh, my gosh!" Alma shrieks and pulls me into a hug. "What the heck, Cat? I've been trying to get ahold of you for the past day. I thought something horrible had happened to you."

"I'm so sorry." I squeeze her tight. "My phone was on silent in my purse. I guess I didn't check it yesterday."

Quinn wraps her arms around the two of us in a three-way hug. "You didn't think you were going to leave the country without a proper goodbye, did you?" she says.

I invite the two of them into my room, thankful I tidied up after the night of sex.

"Seriously, what did you do yesterday? I was so worried about you. I knew the jerk made you come out here to sign, but I thought we'd hang out yesterday since it was your last night," Alma says, disappointment lacing her voice.

I first met Alma when she was dating my ex-husband's brother, Leo. Unlike his brother Stephen, Leo had a heart of gold. Besides my parents, Alma and Leo are another example of true love. I actually waited to finalize my divorce until after Alma's second wedding a couple of weeks ago. I wouldn't have missed it for the world. She's become the sister I never had, and I love her so much.

"It's kind of a crazy story, actually." I look toward my lap, my fingers threading together.

"Oh, my gosh! You hooked up!" Quinn shrieks, clapping her hands together.

"What?" Alma looks from me to Quinn.

My cheeks redden. "I kinda met someone."

"What?" Alma says again, this time with a gasp. "Tell us all about it!"

I shake my head. "It's kind of crazy silly, but I was getting a drink at the bar after I signed the papers. He sat next to me and started talking. He noticed I was bummed, and the day kind of…" I think of the best way to explain it. "…turned into this fun game."

I explain the rules that Bernard came up with and the fake names and the progression of events. Alma and Quinn listen attentively. It's actually quite comical to see how invested in the story they are. For years, I've been the sounding board for their adventures without having any of my own to share.

"So you never found out his real name?" Alma asks.

"No, I only know him as Bernard." I shrug. "All I know is I thought it'd be the worst day of my life, and it turned out to be one of the best. I know it's not like me to be so impulsive and wild, but it felt right."

"Are you kidding?" Quinn asks. "You deserve to be impulsive and wild. You have a lot of shenanigans to make up for. I'm so proud of you."

I chuckle. "Well, I don't know if a one-night stand is something to be proud of."

"No, it is," Quinn disagrees. "You've been trying to make your horrible marriage work for years. You've been surrounded by unhappiness. You, of all people, deserve some fun."

"Seriously." Alma grins. "Good for you, Cat. I'm so relieved you had a great day. I was afraid you were sad and alone."

"I know. It's crazy. I wasn't sad or alone. I still can't believe it. You should've seen us traipsing around the casino hand in hand, making out everywhere like hormonally crazed newlyweds. I should've been embarrassed. I guess it's a good thing I'm leaving the country, so I don't have to show my face down there again." I chuckle.

"No way. You're awesome," Quinn says.

"Absolutely," Alma agrees. "I mean, I'm bummed I didn't get to spend your last day here with you, but I'm so happy it was a good day."

I reach out and squeeze Alma's hand. I know how much she's going to miss me because I'm going to miss her just as much. We've weathered some intense storms together. It's crazy to think she's not going to be a short drive away.

"You'll be back, though?" Quinn asks. "I mean, you have to come back for the wedding."

Quinn got engaged on the beach of Lake Michigan after Alma's wedding.

"Maybe not to live, but I'll definitely be back to visit. There are too many people I love here to stay away for too long. Plus, I wouldn't miss your wedding for anything in the world."

"Okay, good." Quinn seems pleased with my answer.

"Do you have time to go for breakfast before heading to the airport?" Alma questions.

I look at the clock and back at Alma. "I don't. I'm sorry. I wish I did, but I need to get going."

She nods with a small frown on her face. "Okay. At least let us take you. You can give us any more details you think of about your amazing day with Bernard on the way there."

"I'm pretty sure I told you everything." I chuckle.

"Come on, Cat. There must be something you didn't share. We need details. It will be a while until we're together again." Quinn pulls out the handle of my suitcase and pulls it toward the door.

I pick up my purse and carry-on, and quickly scan the room to make sure I didn't leave anything behind. I take a mental picture of the location of Bernard's and my insane honeymoon adventure. With a content smile, I turn away and follow Quinn and Alma out the door.

I entertain the girls with a few more fun tidbits of my time with Bernard in the casino on the way to the airport.

They both agree that they'd pay money to see the outfit I was dared to wear. The comment made me cognizant of the fact that I didn't snap one picture. I never even took my cell out of my purse. I experienced the best day ever and don't have one photo as proof. I suppose that speaks to the true amazingness of the day. I was so immersed and happy, there wasn't a moment when I thought to pull out my cell.

I wish I had a picture to remember him. Bernard was only present for one day of my life, but the impact he had will live on in me forever.

I hug the girls goodbye at the airport and promise to call often. I check my luggage and make my way through security in a timely fashion.

As the plane ascends into the clouds, leaving my home of the past ten years behind, I feel happy. Yes, my marriage was a disaster, but I met and loved so many other wonderful people. The years weren't a waste, and my marriage was a learning experience. I can't regret it because it changed me and made me stronger.

My last day as a resident of Michigan was so beautiful. I couldn't ask for anything more. To my husband for a day, Bernard Peppercakes, I say…thank you. That was quite the sendoff. I'll be forever grateful for it.

CHAPTER 6

ONE YEAR LATER

EVERETT

In an argument about something, Asher and Cassie whisper-shout under one of the tall oak trees to the side of the field. Asher's been my roommate and best friend since our freshman year of college. We were paired together in the dorms at U of M, the University of Michigan, and have been tight since.

Cassie has lived in the apartment across the hall from us for the past six years, and she and her bestie Tannon have become our closest friends.

Tannon moved out and got married earlier this year,

so now it's just the three of us—Asher, Cassie, and me—living in the two apartments above the Starbucks in Ann Arbor. At some point, I know I need to move out of the city, or at least the part of Ann Arbor that houses the university and its students, but it's been fun. Asher and I have had an epic ride.

Our apartment is the location of a big party most Saturday nights, and it's a blast. Sure, my mom wants me to grow up and move out on my own—get married, buy a house, and all that. Someday, I want that all, too. But until I find the woman I'm meant to spend the rest of my life with, it seems pointless to buy a house. Plus, it's insanely convenient that I can roll out of bed and walk down to the coffee shop to conduct business. Seriously, a flight of stairs is all that separates me from delicious coffee and a vibing office space every day.

I work remotely for a tech firm, so all I need is my laptop, and I'm good to go.

Admittedly, many of my friends are growing up and getting married, though I'm not going to mention that to my mother just yet. My gaze follows the small white lights hanging from the roof of the barn. They create a magical and romantic glow.

Our friend Quinn got married today in what she calls a rustic chic vibe, and it's pretty cool. I guess I never really thought about having a wedding in a barn, but it turned out extremely nice.

"Hey," my girlfriend, Lila, hands me a bottle of Blue

Moon, my favorite beer. "Is Quinn really going to slide down that in her wedding dress?"

I chuckle. "I'm sure she is. You know her. She's always up for an adventure."

"I know, but it's her wedding dress."

"Eh." I shrug. "It's wrapping up. I mean, she got through the ceremony with dancing and stuff. She and Ollie probably just want to celebrate in a fun way. It's memorable, right? How many bouncy houses and giant inflatable water slides have you seen at a wedding?"

"Well, none, but that doesn't mean anything." Lila takes a sip of her wine.

"You wanna go down it?" I quirk a brow. "It'll be fun."

"No way." She scoffs. "And don't even think we're having anything like that at our wedding."

I freeze. Her words send panic through my body.

I've only been dating Lila for a few months, and I'm nowhere near imagining us married. I met her in Starbucks when she was studying for her final exams for her senior year of college at U of M. I was working on a client's website, and I noticed her deep in concentration. I watched as she took a sip of her coffee only to realize that she'd already finished it. The little scowl on her face was so damn cute. I went up to the counter and asked for the same coffee that she'd ordered thirty minutes prior and proceeded to deliver it to her. Yep, I'm romantic as hell.

A sad, beautiful woman is my kryptonite. You can all

but guarantee I'm going to get involved if I see one. I can't resist the role of Prince Charming.

I think my need to rescue women started with my mother. My father left us when I was young, so early on that I don't even remember him. Growing up, it was just my mother and me—and whatever loser she was trying to get to love her at the time. It wasn't easy seeing my mom change over and over just to be validated by a man. And boy…could she pick them. Not a decent one in her collective dating history. It was like Groundhog Day of bad relationships, one disaster after the next. They all ended the same way, with my mother's broken heart.

So I made it my job to cheer her up. As certain as the horrendous end of each of her relationships was also the certainty that I'd be there when it was over. I'd be there to make her laugh, spoil her rotten, and remind her that she's loved. If only by me, she's loved.

I'm not going to lie. I've realized since that the role I played took its toll on me. I've never been in love, always breaking it off before it gets that far. I'm aware that it's a pattern with me, yet I continue with it. Spending my entire childhood convincing my mother that my love was enough, only to have her chase after the next piece-of-shit man, left me with some issues. I know my mother loves me, but I can't deny the insecurity she caused in me. Perhaps, it's self-preservation, but I can't imagine anything worse than falling in love with someone only to find out that I'm not enough for them. I've seen that story before, and I have no interest in playing a role.

Yeah, so there's probably some unprocessed shit stirring within me that I should work out with a therapist, but there's no need now, seeing that I'm nowhere near ready to settle down. A memo, that pretty little Lila, should read.

She giggles and then slaps my chest. "Oh, chill out. I'm not saying we're getting married tomorrow or anything."

Or ever, I think on instinct, and the thought takes me aback. Either Lila is marriage material or she's not my happily ever after and I'm continuing to date her and lead her on for…what exactly? Which I suppose also means I'm more messed up than I thought. Either way, I apparently have some issues to deal with.

"What are they arguing about?" Lila motions toward Cassie and Asher. "I have no idea."

I start in their direction, and Lila follows.

"You guys know it's really poor taste to argue at someone's wedding? Right?" I say when we've reached them.

Cassie looks at me. "We're not arguing. We're just talking."

"Okay, sure…" I raise my brows. "Regardless, you should pick up your *talking* another time. Where are your dates anyway?"

"Bennett said something about the bouncy house." Cassie waves toward the white castle-shaped inflatable on the edge of the field beside the water slide.

"Bethany is getting us drinks...I think," Asher says with a shrug.

We start walking toward where the rest of the wedding-goers are congregating by the inflatables.

Tannon leans against a tree. Her baby, who's only a couple of months old, is strapped to her chest.

"Motherhood looks so good on you, Tan," I tell her.

She looks down at her sleeping son. "Thanks."

A moment later, her husband, Jude, is at her side handing her a bottle of water.

"Who is Alma talking to?" Cassie asks.

Alma, the bride's best friend, has her cell up to her ear as she all but shouts into it.

Tannon chuckles. "It's all very interesting. I guess their friend Cat is on her way. She was supposed to be here yesterday, but her plane connection in London was canceled, and it took her a while to get a flight out. Now, she's driving through the country roads and is lost trying to find this place. Oh, and there's some big surprise she has for them."

"This wedding is just full of surprises, isn't it?" Cassie shoots a glare toward Asher.

"What does that mean?" Tannon questions her best friend.

"Nothing," Cassie grumbles before mouthing, "I'll tell you later."

"There's nothing to tell," Asher grumbles.

I exchange glances with Lila, and she shrugs.

"So who's going down the water slide?" Jude asks.

"I might. I mean, how many times can you say you've been down a huge inflatable water slide at a wedding?" Asher says.

"Yeah, I think I will, too. There's something sexy about being all wet, right? I think Bennett would appreciate it later." Cassie eyes Asher.

"Cassie!" Tannon exclaims. "What is going on with you? Spill it."

"Nothing," Cassie says with an air of innocence. "Bennett just likes it when I'm wet."

Lila looks at me, her eyes wide. She looks completely uncomfortable with this entire conversation. She hasn't been in the group long enough to know that crude conversations are normal with us.

Alma goes running by us, yelling, "Oh my gosh!"

Quinn, in her wet wedding dress, wraps herself in a towel and runs past us. "She's here!" She giggles.

A group of people surrounds the friend, who, from the conversations I've heard, hasn't been home for a while. There's a round of gasps and cheers and all sorts of excited voices talking over one another.

"I feel like we're missing out," Cassie says. "Let's go check it out." She nods toward the commotion.

Lila loops her arm through mine and leans her face against my bicep as we walk. She really is a sweet person and beautiful inside and out. Maybe I should figure out how to get over my issues sooner than later. I bend down and kiss the top of her head, and she looks at me and smiles.

We approach Quinn and friends, and a shiver runs down my spine. A faint air of familiarity comes over me when I catch a brief snippet of a voice I recognize or more so an accent. It's the accent of someone from afar who's lived in the United States a long time, and from a young enough age that the English is almost perfect… but there's a faint nod to the country's dialect she learned first.

I step toward the circle, and my mouth falls open when I see her. She's just as beautiful as I remember. I never thought I'd see her again, and she's here—at Quinn's fancy farm wedding of all places.

She's smiling and laughing with her friends. It takes her a moment to notice me, but there's no denying the moment she does. Her grin falters, and her big uniquely green eyes widen in shock. Her light brown hair is longer than the last time I saw her. It falls over her shoulders, landing a couple inches past her chest.

She swallows. "Bernard?"

"Daisy?" My voice quivers.

Quinn looks from me to Daisy, who I guess is named Cat.

"That's Bernard?" Quinn shrieks, pointing at me.

Cat nods.

"Everett is your Bernard? Your casino husband?" Quinn clarifies.

Cat nods again, her eyes not leaving me.

"Oh my gosh." Alma gasps.

"What does she mean casino husband?" Lila tugs on my arm, but I ignore her.

Alma hands a baby to Cat, and I stare at the little girl in Cat's arms. She's not much older than Tannon's baby, maybe three or four months—not that I'm an expert at guessing baby ages. Wow, Daisy—I mean, Cat—has a kid. The baby is at the age where I only know it's a girl because Cat has a lace headband with a bow wrapped around the baby's head—that, and she's wearing a poufy pink dress.

"You're a mom?" I ask. There's so much I want to say and ask, but those three words are all I can get out.

Cat swallows. "Yeah, her name is Bernadette Daisy."

CHAPTER 7

CAT

So many emotions are swirling inside my chest. I can't believe this is real, and he's here—my Bernard, or I suppose Everett.

He looks like an Everett—tall, beautiful, and good. I've met him in my dreams almost every night since returning to Moscow. I prayed I'd find him someday but had no idea how. To see him—here, among my friends—is unreal.

Everett stands stiff, blinking. His eyes dart from our daughter to me and back again.

"Yeah, I think we should get back to the inflatable fun, guys. I mean, there's no line," a guy I don't know calls out to the group. He squeezes Everett's shoulder, a reassuring smile on his face. He must be a good friend. I wonder if he's the guy who left him at the casino to hook up with the blackjack dealer.

What a small world. It's crazy to think that we're all connected and meeting here at the tail end of Quinn's wedding.

"E," the girl on Everett's arm whines. Her worried gaze begs for his attention.

"Give me a minute, please," he says to her without taking his eyes from me.

The others whisper to each other and slowly disperse, leaving just the three of us.

"We should probably talk," I say.

"Yeah, I think that'd be a good idea." His voice is flat, void of the energy I remember.

There's an uneasiness in the pit of my stomach. He wipes his palms on his suit pant legs as he steps past me.

He leads us to a barn that's beautifully decorated with small white twinkle lights and an abundance of flowers. Stepping to the side of the large door, he motions me in and slides the heavy barn door shut.

A beautiful floral arch straight out of a princess movie is set up at one end of the barn, which is surely where Quinn and Ollie said their vows. I would've loved to see the wedding. My annoyance toward the airline that canceled my flight grows, but what's done is done. There are more pressing issues at hand.

We take a seat by the floral arch. The bench is

constructed from an actual tree sliced in half—rustic and gorgeous all at once.

Everett looks at our baby. "She's mine?"

"She is."

"I don't understand." His voice trembles.

"I guess your casino bathroom condoms weren't of the highest caliber." My joke falls flat.

He shakes his head. "I have a daughter? Why didn't you find me?" his stunning hazels fill with unshed tears.

"I couldn't. Of course, I tried, but I knew nothing about you, not even a name. I called the casino and asked if I could get copies of the names on the credit card receipts from the bar that day, but that was a no-go. The room was in my name. I had nothing to go on. I wanted to contact you the moment I woke up and found you gone, but it was impossible. The no-truths rule really messed things up."

"How stupid," he chastises under his breath. "What was I thinking with that whole game?"

"I can guarantee that you weren't thinking you'd have a child from it." I attempt another joke, still so confused as to what he's thinking or feeling.

He tilts his head, and a sweet grin finds his face as he takes Bernadette in. "How old is she?"

"Three months."

"I've missed three months of her life?" He sounds distraught, and it catches me off guard.

"I'm sorry."

"Can I hold her?" His desperate stare breaks my heart. I wasn't sure how he'd react, but he's clearly upset.

I hold her out to him. "Of course."

He takes her in his arms, his expression one of wonder.

"I call her Benny or Benny Baby as a nickname. Bernadette sounds so mature for such a little thing. You know?"

He runs a finger over her short wispy blond hair, a smile coming to his face. "She's so beautiful. She has your eyes."

I nod. "She does, and your blond hair and full lips."

"And your cute little button nose." He lightly presses his finger against the tip of her nose. "I can't believe we made her. She's so perfect!" He pulls his gaze from Benny and holds my stare. "You must've been so shocked."

"I was. There was a moment of devastation." I force a strained chuckle. "But that didn't last long. I had wanted a change. I had already retired from modeling, and I got divorced and moved back to Moscow. So why not add another change to the mix? I guess, I figured it was meant to be. And having her now…I know it was. I've never loved anyone more."

His demeanor hardens. "You live in Moscow?"

Pulling in a breath, I nod.

"That's so far away." He turns his attention to Benny and lightly squeezes her wrist rolls, which, admittedly, I'm obsessed with, too. "I want to be in her life."

"Well, I'm here for a couple of weeks. You can see her and get to know her, and we can discuss the future."

"I grew up without a father, Dai—Cat," he stumbles over my name. "I would never want my child to grow up without me. I would never abandon her. Now that I know about her..." His words trail off as he runs the back of his finger across her cheek.

I'm beyond grateful that destiny brought us together again. I've prayed for this moment. I wanted so badly to find this man and tell him that we made a beautiful baby girl. I guess I just never thought about what would happen if I actually found him. I had no idea what his reaction would be or how it would change my life with Benny. A sudden and unexpected panic chills my veins. *I can't be without her. She's mine. What if he wants to split custody?* I'd die if I could only see her half the year. *No.*

Everett reaches out a hand and touches mine. "I would never take her from you. Ever!" he reassures me. My panic must be written all over me.

I swallow hard and quiet the irrational part of my brain telling me to head to the airport now and leave the country. He can't take her if we're an ocean apart. The reality is I don't know this man. We had a brief encounter built on lies and lust, and I don't know anything real about him. Yet, at the same time, I feel I can trust him. For whatever reason, I do. He seems genuinely kind, and I pray my instinct isn't wrong.

I bite my lip. "I'm sorry. I just…I don't know you, but I know I would die before I let anything happen to her."

"You know me. Maybe not the specific details of my life, but the core of who I am, you know," he says. "I would never do anything to hurt you or her. I simply want to be a part of her life. I think that's only fair. You don't owe me anything. You could fly back to Moscow, and there's probably not anything I could do about it. However, just imagine if the roles were reversed. What if you missed the first three months of her life and just found her. Wouldn't you want to know her, too?"

"Yeah," I admit. My heart sinks, realizing how much more complicated my life has suddenly become.

"Okay, this got really deep, really fast. Let's back up. You're here for two weeks. Let's just spend time together and figure it out," he says as Benny starts fussing.

"I think she's hungry," I say, extending my arms to take her.

"Oh, okay." He hands her over to me.

I lay Benny in my arm and pull the bodice of my dress down and position my breast in front of her mouth. She latches on like she hasn't eaten in days like she always does. This little lady loves to eat.

"Holy hell." Everett groans and looks away. "Why is that turning me on?"

"Oh my gosh. Are you twelve?" I laugh. "She's eating."

He rubs his temples. "Yeah, apparently, I am. I know it's natural and all that, but I got sudden flashbacks to our night together. Do you ever think about it?"

"Only every day," I say truthfully.

"Yeah, it was great. Right?" He grins playfully.

"It was," I admit with a squint. "We always agreed it was just a one-day adventure. Plus, things are different now. I'm a mother. I've moved on. Benny and I have a whole life in Moscow. And… don't you have a girlfriend?" I think about the woman clinging to his arm moments ago.

"Yeah, I guess I do," he says as if he just remembered that fact. "Do you…I mean, are you with anyone?"

"No. It's just Benny and me. I haven't been with anyone since you." I shoot him a mock glare. "Not that it's any of your business."

"Of course not." He raises his hands in surrender. "Though you have to admit that night was pretty memorable."

"It was, for sure. But it wasn't real," I remind him.

"I don't know about you, but the sex felt pretty real to me." He smirks, and the hormone-frenzied butterflies return.

"We have chemistry, I'll give you that. But we don't know each other," I say.

I'm so confused. I can't tell if Everett is implying something, flirting, or just stating his opinion. Truthfully, I have no idea. We're nothing to each other but a day of fun and a one-night stand that led to a child. What is the etiquette here? Do we build a friendship? Try to date?

A part of me is afraid to truly get to know Everett because I've built him and that magical day up in my mind for the past year. I'd hate for reality to shine an unflattering light. If I'm being honest, I'd come to terms with never knowing who Bernard really was. I felt fortunate to have him in my dreams because there he'd always be perfect.

One thing is for certain. That day changed my life in more ways than one. I'm not the same woman I was when he found me sulking over my martini, and I'll never be that woman again. The Cat of a year ago needed his strength and his humor to pick me up, to make me feel okay. Now, I can do that on my own. I know who I am and what I want…and I built it for myself and my daughter.

I don't need him or any man to be happy. I found the key to the most beautiful life, and I'm holding her in my arms.

CHAPTER 8

CAT

*A*lma sets a cup of tea in front of me.
"Thank you," I say.
Her five-year-old daughter, Love, is upstairs riffling through her toy chest to find all the dolls she doesn't play with to give to Benny.

We hear a loud noise and a crash resembling a box of fallen Legos. "That should be fun cleaning up later. You know, she's going to come down with dozens of dolls." Alma chuckles.

"She's going to be a great big sister someday," I offer.

Alma nods. "Yeah, she is …someday." I don't miss the sadness in her voice. She and her husband, Amos, have been trying to conceive since before their wedding two years ago. "It happened once, so it can happen again, right?"

"Of course, and I have no doubt it will." I take a sip of the tea.

"But enough about me. I need to know everything. I didn't want to bombard you with too many questions last night, but… Oh. Em. Gee, Cat. There's so much I want to know. First of all, like why didn't you tell me?" There's an air of hurt in her voice.

"I'm so sorry about that, I am. I guess the truth is that I was trying to make sense of it all. I spent my pregnancy soul-searching and figuring out who I was going to be as a mother, and I needed to do it on my own."

"Well, you were clearly one of those women who gain no additional weight, other than your belly, because I saw no sign of it when we spoke over video chat every week for a year."

"Yeah, my mother says it's my height. *I was born to carry children*, she loved to tell me." I drop my eyes to the baby carrier at my feet where Benny sleeps. "They love her so much, my parents. She's just…perfect."

Alma smiles and nods her head. "I know what you mean. You can talk about a mother's love for her child over and over, but others don't truly understand unless they've been a parent themselves. You know?"

"I do."

"What does Everett think of all this?" she asks.

"I guess he wants to be a part of her life." A frown graces my face.

Alma narrows her eyes. "Well, that's good…right?"

"Yeah, I don't know." I blow out a breath of air. "Yes, I'm glad that Benny's father is a noble and decent person, but it changes things. I feel fiercely protective of her, and the thought of someone else having a say in her life worries me. I never thought I'd see him again, to be fair. The entire pregnancy and first months of her life, it's been me—loving her and figuring out what our life is going to look like. Now? It's all messed up. Everett is an entirely new variable that changes everything. It terrifies me."

"Yeah, I get that. I really do. It's always just been Love and me. I understand the fierce protectiveness you feel." She looks at Bernadette, and a knowing smile graces her face.

I'm sure Alma understands more than anyone how I'm feeling.

"How do you know Everett anyway?" I ask.

"Well, he and Asher are friends with and live in the apartment across from Tannon and Cassie who Quinn is close with. I don't hang out with them a lot, but Tannon and Cassie have taken many of the self-defense courses at The Lair." Alma talks of the organization that she built with her late husband. The Lair helps people, especially the troubled teens, in the community. "And Tannon is now married to the guy who instructs those self-defense classes. The few times I've hung out with that group, Everett seemed like a good guy. I still can't believe he's your epic one-day adventure." She chuckles.

"I know, it's crazy. And I feel like he's a good guy, too. But I did marry Stephen…so, maybe I'm not the best judge of character." I force a laugh.

"Well, everyone is entitled to a mistake here and there. Plus, if you didn't marry Stephen, I wouldn't know you, and that would be a true tragedy. God, I've missed you!" she exclaims. "These two weeks are going to fly by."

"They are." I groan. "Especially now that I have baby daddy issues to deal with."

Love comes barreling down the stairs, her arms full of dolls. "I got some!" she yells, and I look down to Benny.

"Shh, quiet, Lovey. The baby's still sleeping," Alma reminds her.

"Sorry," Love whispers. Stopping in front of me, she drops a pile of princess dolls on my lap. She has quite the obsession with Disney princesses.

"Oh, my gosh, Lovey! You're giving all these to the baby?"

"Yeah, I want her to have them." She grins proudly.

"That's so sweet." I lean toward her and give her a kiss on her head. "You're the best. I've missed you so much. I can't believe how big you are."

"I know. Gigi says I'm growing like a weed." Love states proudly.

"Well, you are. Where is Gigi?" I ask.

"With her boyfriend." Love grins wide.

I look at Alma.

"Yeah, she and Luca are in love," Alma says. "They're doing really well, and Mom is…good."

"Mom?" I quirk a brow. In all the time I've known Alma, she's always referred to her mother by her first name, Lee-Anne. Her mother wasn't the best growing up. It's a miracle that Alma turned out as well as she did.

"Yeah. We're all trying to do better, right?"

"I guess we are. What are you doing without all her delicious, healthy meals?" I tease.

Alma's mother follows a plant-based, no salt, no oil, no sugar diet and loves to cook for others. Because I follow a mostly plant-based diet, especially back when I was modeling, I enjoyed Lee-Anne's meals. Everyone else, though? Not so much.

"Daddy cooks now," Love says. "And his food is so yummy but don't tell Gigi. I don't want to hurt her feelings."

I chuckle. "I won't, and your daddy is a great cook." I look toward my lap full of plush princesses. "So tell me who everyone is."

Love picks up a doll in a purple dress. "This is Rapunzel. She's from *Tangled*, and Benny is going to love her. She's one of my favorites."

"Oh, my gosh! You've grown like ten years since I've been gone," I exclaim. The last time I was here, Love was calling the princess Punzel. "You can say your 'r' sounds now?"

Alma shakes her head. "I know. Darn school. She's losing her baby voice completely. I hate it."

Love laughs. "Mommy always says that."

"Okay, so who else do we have?" I ask.

Love picks up each plush princess and tells me her name and which Disney movie she's from in exciting detail. She's so beautiful and looks so much like her biological father. It hurts my heart that she's grown so much, and I missed it. A year is such a long time in the life of a child.

"You know what?" I say to Love. "Benny is going to adore all these baby princess dolls. But we can't take them all back because we just won't have the space in our luggage. So why don't you hold on to them here so Benny can play with them when we visit. Maybe, just pick one that you want her to take with her, okay?"

"Just one to take on the plane?" Love clarifies.

"Right." I nod. "The rest you can keep safe for her until we come back. Which one do you think she will like the most?"

Love looks at the dolls and holds one up for me. "Mommy always says that Snow White was my first love. So maybe she can be Benny's too?"

Alma's body language changes, and I know what

she's feeling. Love's obsession with Snow White was during a very emotional time in Alma's life. I can all but guarantee that this well-loved plushie holds all sorts of important memories for Alma.

"I think you should keep Snow White." I smile toward Love. "It's important to hold on to the ones we love the most."

"I know, but I want Benny to be able to love her, too." Love lowers her stare.

She has such a kind heart.

"Okay, then why don't we take a shopping trip to the mall while I'm home. We can stop at the Disney store and get Benny her own little Snow White. That way you can both have her. Does that sound good?"

Love presses her lips together in thought. "Okay. That works!"

"Great! Now, go put these somewhere safe." I motion toward the dolls.

Love swoops her arms over my lap and holds them against her chest. She takes off, dolls in tow, up the stairs.

"Thank you." Alma grins.

"No worries."

"So when are you meeting up with Everett?"

I glance at the time on my cell. "In a couple of hours. He said he had some stuff to take care of this morning."

"What are you going to tell him?" she asks.

I shake my head. "I have no idea."

Last night during our talk at the wedding, Everett asked if we could get together this afternoon. Shortly after we emerged from the barn to a group of curious friends, he and his date left. I could barely sleep last night because all the scenarios of what our conversation today could bring were running through my head. I have no idea what's in store for me today. In the brief time I've known Everett, the one thing I can count on is it's going to be completely unpredictable. Which is what scares me.

CHAPTER 9

EVERETT

*L*ila storms out of the apartment but not before screaming a slur of choice words in my direction. In hindsight, perhaps bringing her back to the apartment last night wasn't the best idea. But dropping her off after arriving home late from a wedding and quickly ending it in the car didn't feel like a great option either.

To be fair, I didn't think we were that serious. At a few months, I suppose she was one of my longest relationships, so it's possible she was more invested than me.

I feigned exhaustion last night and pretended to fall fast asleep, so Lila wouldn't want any post-wedding sex.

Normally, I'd be all about it. Nothing is a better aphrodisiac to a woman than a wedding, am I right? Non-married women—hell, probably even happily married women—eat that shit up. A celebration of love is a turn-on. And, on most days, I would've taken full advantage.

Things are different now.

All I can think about is her. The dream I was lucky to have for one day, the fantasy that has been front and center on my highlight reel of life over the past year is back. It's unreal. And…the two of us made a kid…a real baby. *Mind blown.*

I have to be honest in saying this is not how I thought my journey into fatherhood would go. Getting to know my daughter when she lives halfway around the world with my one-night stand presents its own set of challenges. It's not ideal, not by a long shot. I've always been careful. Wearing a condom—regardless of whether a woman says she's on birth control—is my religion. *Fucking cheap-ass casino condoms.*

Whatever. It's done. There's an adorable baby with my DNA, and therefore—I'm a father, which is not something I take lightly.

I didn't plan on becoming a father for many years. However, I always knew that when I became one, I'd be awesome. I know what it's like to grow up without one, and my child will never know what that feels like.

The fact that my daughter lives four thousand, eight hundred, and forty-four miles away from me is a major complication. How do I know the exact number? Well, it's the first thing I googled. The second was airfare to Moscow, and I'll just say flying over there monthly is not ideal unless I start making a hell of a lot more money.

Which leads me to the plan.

Make Cat stay.

How can I make her stay? She has a life over there, family...probably a new career. These are all things I'm sure we'll discuss today. Yet she's lived here before. She moved here for love, and if she did it once, she'll do it again. *I hope.* So the plan, in a nutshell, is to make her fall in love with me.

It's not crazy. We have chemistry. Our day together was so much fun. Surely, two people that in tune with one another have a promising future. Am I in love with her? No. How could I be? I've literally spent one day and an hour in her presence. But I am insanely attracted to her, so that has to count for something. Maybe I'm dreaming, but I feel I could love her and her me.

I've never been in love. A wall was built around my heart a long time ago, something—until recently—I hadn't even realized I'd done. It makes sense after watching my mother and her disaster of relationships over the years. It's time to break those walls down, and if anyone can do that, it's Cat, the mother of my baby girl.

"Wow. So it's over with Lila?" my roommate Asher asks.

"Yeah. I wasn't feeling it." I grab a bottle of water from the refrigerator.

"Okay, well, now that she's gone, I need some details. So Quinn's friend Cat is your casino goddess? The woman you've talked up so much I thought you might be making her up?" He chuckles.

I shake my head with a scoff. "That's her. You'll never believe what I found out last night? She was a supermodel. I told you she was incredible."

"And you're a *dad*?"

"I know. Like, what the fuck? It's crazy, right? I can't believe it…" My voice trails off as I lift the water bottle to my lips.

"What are you going to do?" he asks.

"I want to be part of my daughter's life, obviously. I mean, she wasn't planned, but that doesn't change the fact that she's mine."

"Right. Right." Asher nods.

"Yet she lives on another continent. So I don't know how that will work. I'm going to talk it over with her mom today."

Asher blows out a breath. "That's heavy."

"Tell me about it. But I was up most of the night thinking about everything. She's staying with Alma for two weeks. So that's the amount of time I have to make her fall in love with me."

"What!" Asher shouts, his eyes wide. "You're in love with her?"

"Not yet, but I will be."

"Man, I get it. You had a shitty dad and a messed-up mom. You crave something normal, but you can't just decide to fall in love with someone. That's not how it works. Plus, you really can't predict her feelings. I think you're setting yourself up for failure. Maybe you should focus on how the logistics of seeing your daughter will work."

"I know it sounds insane. All I can say is you weren't there. You didn't see what we had that day. There's something between us—something real. I feel it. Now that we have a kid together, it's worth the leap of faith. If it doesn't work out, it doesn't, but I must try. I can be as optimistic as I want about my relationship with my daughter, but you know damn well that if she grows up in Moscow, we won't be close."

"Well, I hope you get what you want, E," Asher says. He grabs the pull-up bar mounted to the doorframe and starts pulling himself up. The guy loves to work out. He has a professional career as a personal trainer, so I get his need to keep in shape. But it's a lot.

I toss the empty water bottle into the recycling bin. "What was going on with you and Cassie last night?"

"Nothing." He breathes out between reps.

I shake my head. "Oh, it wasn't nothing."

"It really was. She was just mad at me for something.

I barely remember. We'd both taken advantage of the open bar at the wedding and were arguing over something stupid. So what's your plan for today, *Romeo?*" he asks.

"I have no idea," I say with a groan. "I'm picking Cat and the baby up from Alma's house, and that's as far as I've gotten. I could barely sleep last night trying to make a plan. Obviously, I want her to fall for me, so she and my baby stay, but I'm still trying to figure out how to accomplish that."

Asher lets go of the bar and drops to the ground. "Listen, man, the only way this will work is if she actually falls for you…the real you. Anything else is doomed for failure. So just be yourself. You guys had this magical day together, but that's not reality. You need her to fall for the everyday you. I'm heading into work. Why don't you bring her and the baby by and just hang out and talk?"

"Maybe." I don't sound so sure.

"What are you going to do? Whisk her off on a hot air balloon ride while Ed Sheeran's 'Perfect' serenades her from portable speakers, and you toss rose petals at her feet?" He laughs at his own joke.

"A hot air balloon was on the list of possibilities." I squint.

"Keep it simple. Seriously. You're awesome, and if she doesn't see that, it's on her."

"Thanks for the pep talk, man." I chuckle.

"Anytime. So what are we thinking for Saturday's party?" he asks.

Asher and I have been throwing a Saturday night apartment party pretty much every week since we graduated. We're the eternal college frat boys. Thinking about it now, maybe it's not the coolest thing to be.

"Count me out for the next couple of weeks," I tell him. "I'll be busy doing the dad thing."

"God, that's still so hard to comprehend," he says as he heads toward his bedroom.

"Tell me about it."

CHAPTER 10

CAT

Given that it's summer, I haven't seen as many college students in this part of Ann Arbor, but quite a few are still rushing by. I'm sure the fact that we're standing in front of the most popular coffee spot in town helps lure the young learners in.

This town is known as the home of the University of Michigan, and though most of my best friends live here, they don't reside in the part of the city that's on campus.

"Well, mi hija, this is your daddy's place." I eye the Starbucks and then look up to the windows above, wondering if his apartment faces the street or the back alley. "We should go in, yes?" I say to Bernadette.

I scoop up her car seat carrier, holding the handle in

the crook of my arm. As per Everett's instructions, I walk around the side of the building until I've reached the entry door in the alley.

He offered to pick the baby and me up from Alma's house, but I chose to meet him at his place instead. I'm still uneasy about this whole situation—not about him, exactly—but the circumstances surrounding us. I wanted to be able to leave when I wanted, so I borrowed Alma's car. A trait of mine that's only intensified over this past year is my need to be in control in all aspects of my life.

Pulling the handle of the glass door, I step in and start up the stairs. The stairwell is nice enough, but what did I expect? This is Ann Arbor, after all. Most places in this town are decent. Once I reach the top, there are two doors. I inhale a deep breath and lift my fist, ready to knock on his. Only, before I gain the courage to knock, he's swinging the door wide open. His smile wide.

"Hey! It's my two favorite girls. Come in." He steps to the side to allow me entry.

"Were you stalking that peephole?" I look at the door.

He quirks a brow. "Would you judge me if I was?"

I shake my head. "Not at all."

His place, or I suppose the place he shares with his roommate, is nice. It's clean with modern furniture. The décor is simple but elegant for a bachelor pad.

"It's not much. I know. Had I known I was a dad, I'd

have grown up and moved off campus this past year." He makes a joke at his own expense.

"No, it's nice. Is your roommate here?" I set the carrier down and bend to unbuckle Benny.

Everett retreats to the kitchen and retrieves a bottle of water from the refrigerator. "No, he's working. He's a personal trainer. He has some preseason sessions with some of the Detroit Lion's players today. Do you follow football?"

I chuckle. "Not even a little."

"Well, I guess that will be our thing, huh, Benny?" He takes her hand in his and rubs his thumb over her skin.

I clear my throat, swallowing the lump of emotion. "So what do you have planned today?"

He scrunches his lips and narrows his eyes. I can imagine him making this face as a little boy after he just got caught doing something bad.

"Um...this." He lifts his shoulders and bites his bottom lip, and a flashback from our day at the casino surfaces.

"Oh," I say, startled. "Right. Perfect."

"I guess I thought it'd be nice to just hang out and get to know each other?"

"Of course." I scoff at my own idiocy. "That really is great. I don't know. Given the little I know about you from our day in Detroit, I thought you'd have some elaborate thing planned, like a horse-drawn carriage ride or something. You just seemed like that type of guy."

He laughs, a loud boisterous sound. "Well"—he shrugs—"a hot air balloon ride was an initial option, but Asher told me to be chill and spend today just getting to know you and Benny."

"He sounds like a smart guy." I follow Everett over to the leather sofa.

"Eh, he has his moments."

We take a seat, and Everett asks to hold Benny. His face lights up as he brings her to his lap.

"What do you want to know?" I ask.

"Well, for starters. How about names? What's your whole name? What's hers? Where are you from? Where do you live? What do you do? All of it. I want to know all of it," he blurts out in rapid succession.

His big hazel eyes appear less green than I remember. In this light, they're a light shade of brown with golden stripes. It's fascinating to me how the tint of his irises change the way they do. He really is a gorgeous man. If I was going to get knocked up by a stranger, he was a good choice. The two of us made a beautiful baby.

"Caterina Avilova Araya is my name. The Avilova comes from my father. His surname is Avilov, but in Russia, last names are gender-specific. So the female version adds an a at the end. Then Araya is my mother's last name, the one she got from her father. It's Spanish."

"So your parents are from Russia and Spain?"

I nod. "Yes, my parents met in Spain when my mother was a teen. She was my father's server. Apparently, it was love at first sight. I believe it because to this day, they are still very much in love. My father brought my mother and her parents to Moscow with him after they were married. He runs a business there. It's all very technical, but it's an investment firm, more or less. My mother and her parents started a Spanish restaurant which they still run."

"So you speak Spanish and Russian?" he asks before playfully chomping on Benny's fingers with his lips causing her to grin.

"I do, and French, German, and of course English."

"So five languages? Wow."

I shrug. "If you start young, it's really not that difficult. I picked them up fairly quickly, I think."

"So what is Benny's entire name?"

"I told you about the Bernadette Daisy, and then she has the same surnames as me."

"So Bernadette Daisy Avilova Araya?" he says slowly.

"Exactly." I sense a slight sadness or maybe just disappointment in his expression as he looks at Benny. "I didn't know your last name."

"It's fine. It's West, Everett West."

"Oh, that's nice. Well, if she were to incorporate your name, it'd be Bernadette West Avilova. In Spain, the father's surname is first, and the mother's father—the grandfather's—surname is second. The grandmother's name gets dropped."

"West-Avilova. It has a nice ring to it," he offers.

"It's not bad," I tease.

"So what else?"

I tell him about my family in Moscow. I'm an only child, but my father has many siblings, and therefore, I have tons of cousins in the area. Truthfully, I missed them all—my aunts and uncles, cousins, and a bunch of little second cousins running around. Every couple of months, my mom shuts the restaurant down early, and my dad's entire family shows up. My aunties take over the restaurant's kitchen, where they prepare pelmeni, Borshch Moskovsky, and blini. It's an all-night celebration with lots of vodka. They're all loud and crazy…and so much fun.

Everett kisses Benny on the head and hands her over to me. "Speaking of food. I'm making dinner."

"You are?" I raise a brow. "Well, that's exciting. What are you making?"

"I remember you telling me that you're a plant-based eater. There's this restaurant in town that serves this quinoa bowl that's incredibly good, and that's saying something coming from someone who loves a juicy steak. I looked on Pinterest and found a recipe I thought was similar. I'm going to try to replicate it. I can't promise that it'll be great, but I'll give it a go." He pulls a saucepan from a cupboard and fills it with water. After placing it on the stove, he retrieves a cutting board and some vegetables.

I can't deny that it warms my heart that he remembered such a little detail about me from a simple conversation a year ago. Add in the fact that he searched Pinterest for recipes, and it's cuteness overload. Stephen was never so thoughtful. I shake my head and clear my thoughts. I promised myself that I wouldn't allow my ex any more space in my thoughts. For the most part, I've been doing great forgetting him altogether. It's hard not to compare Everett to him when I'm in a dating situation.

Is that what we're doing? Dating?

No, we're just getting to know each other for Benny's sake. That's all.

Benny starts to fuss, so I take a seat on the barstool facing the kitchen and nurse her while watching Everett. He's sexy as hell in the kitchen. What is it about a man who can cook that's such a turn-on?

"So tell me about the dishes your family loves…Pelamenini?"

"Pelmini." I smile. 'They're like a mix between dumplings and pierogis. They're usually filled with meat and then slathered in sour cream. Of course, vodka is the drink of choice when they're on the menu. The Borshch Moskovsky is like a…beet soup with cabbage and beef, and then blini are thin pancakes, like crepes, and they're also eaten with sour cream."

He scoops up the halved cherry tomatoes from the cutting board and drops them into a bowl. "You know, I don't see you eating any of that."

I laugh. "Yeah, it's on the heavy and meaty side for my taste. I mean, I'm not as strict with my diet now that I'm not modeling, but I haven't eaten like that since I was a child, and truthfully—I don't miss it. I like vegetables and whole grains. I feel good when I eat them. It's always been about health for me, more so than weight management, I guess."

"So what do you eat there?" he asks.

"It's the same as here really. Good food can be found anywhere. I just have to look for it or ask the chef to make substitutions. My mother's restaurant specializes in Spanish food, right? Well, she makes the best gazpacho. You guys have it here in places, but nothing here holds a candle to my mother's. It's like a cold tomato soup with lots of garlic. Delicious. My mother also makes a veggie seafood paella for the restaurant, and she'll make me a batch without the seafood. Otherwise, it's like normal. I buy fruits and vegetables from the store. It's not too complicated." I chuckle. "Everyone has always been so fascinated by what I eat. I can guarantee you that I've never starved."

"People are interested because it takes a lot of effort. It's much easier to pick up a burger and fries from a fast-food line." The way in which he's peeling and cutting the garlic so quickly tells me that he's not new to cooking.

"It's just how I live my life, so it's normal." I narrow my gaze. "I don't think you're getting your meals from a fast-food line, either. You know how to cook."

He grins. "Yeah, I cook a lot. Asher's really into his health, so we don't eat a lot of junk. He likes to save his extra calories for Saturday nights, anyway."

"What goes on Saturday night?" I question.

Everett's eyes dart from me to Benny and back to me. "Well, we usually have a big party."

"It's fine." I laugh. "I'm not judging you."

"I already told Asher I'm out for the next two weekends, if you were wondering," he says.

"Good to know." I shake my head, and the corner of my mouth tilts up.

Benny falls asleep against my shoulder. I tap her back gently for a few more minutes before laying her down in her carrier.

I join Everett at the dining table where he's set our quinoa veggie bowls and a glass of red wine.

"Looks amazing," I admit.

"Hopefully, it's edible." He smirks.

"I'm sure it will be."

The meal is delicious, and the company is even better. Everett makes me feel good. I'm content, and carefree when I'm with him. He brought that quality to me a year ago, and it still possesses that magic now. He's simply easy to get along with. He's funny, charming, and so easy on the eyes.

The conversation over dinner is effortless. We talk about our childhoods, favorite movies, and pet peeves. We both agree that people who constantly try to one-up you or interrupt you are the worst.

Before I know it, hours have passed, and my cheeks hurt from smiling. It's the best non-date first date I've ever had, and all we did was talk.

Benny starts to cry. "She probably needs her diaper changed."

"Let me do it," Everett offers. "I should learn, right?"

"Sure." I follow him into the living room. He picks up Benny and lays her on the sofa.

I hand him the supplies and watch as he changes her diaper. He does well, not that it's really all that complicated. But still…his excitement, as if he just accomplished something big, is adorable.

"Good job." I chuckle.

"See? I'm a natural." He leans in and blows a raspberry on Benny's belly. "Aren't I, Benny girl?"

Benny gives him her cutest giggle. She's always super happy when she wakes up from a nap. Everett grabs his cell from the side table and snaps some pictures of her. He picks her up and takes a couple of selfies of them together.

"Get in here, Momma!" he says to me.

I lean in against his shoulder as he snaps some pictures of the three of us.

"Man, we're a good-looking bunch." He shoots me a grin.

"We are," I agree. "Can you send those to me?" We exchanged cell numbers at the wedding last night.

"Absolutely."

I press my lips in a line. "We should probably get going."

Everett's face falls but only for a second. "Okay. I'll see you tomorrow, right?"

I nod. "Yeah, and thanks for today. It was wonderful. Dinner was incredible, and the company was even better."

"I agree." He kisses Benny on the cheeks and buckles her into her car seat carrier. "Thanks for doing this."

"Of course," I respond.

He stands and takes a step toward me. He's so close I can feel the rise and fall of his chest against mine. I look up into his eyes. "Thirteen more days–" I start to speak, but he places his finger against my lips. "I see the wheels turning in your head. Don't make any decisions yet. You promised me two weeks, so I have thirteen more days. Keep an open mind until then."

I nod, my heart picks up speed. My tongue yearns to peek out of my lips and lick his finger, and that urge startles me. Everett's right. My mind has been working on overtime this entire time. The doubts and what-ifs of our situation scream loudly in my head.

With one simple touch of his finger, I want to melt into him. What is it about this man that I can't resist?

He drops his finger and leans in. On an inhale, I close my eyes and wait. He reaches for Benny's carrier, and I snap my eyes open, feeling like an idiot.

He gives me a knowing smile. "I'll see you two tomorrow."

CHAPTER 11

EVERETT

I feel good about yesterday. A day getting to know each other is exactly what we needed. We have sexual chemistry, but that's not up for debate. We obviously have a daughter together. Yet it's the whole question of whether we are compatible on a day-to-day basis. I think we are. From the first moment I met her, I thought we were. But if she wants me to convince her—I'll convince her.

I got up early today and finished the work I had to do for my clients. The cool thing about my job is it's portable and flexible. Items need to be completed, but the when and the where are up to me. It's just noon, and the rest of my day is free.

Slowing my Honda Civic to a stop, I pull into Alma and Amos's driveway. From the intel I've done, Cat used to be married to Alma's late husband's brother, who was a millionaire. I'd bet money that she didn't drive a Honda Civic. Not that she needed her ex's money, anyway. As a supermodel, she's wealthy in her own right. I don't get the impression from Cat that she's materialistic. Well, except for her clothes. Every outfit I've seen her wear has cost more than my rent, I'm sure of it. But seriously, Hondas are reliable with good gas mileage. Surely, I'll get points for my good sense.

Cat exits the front door of the house as soon as I pull up as if she was watching for me. It makes me hopeful. I can't help but smile when I see her outfit. As always, she's as hot as fuck but completely overdressed.

I step out and jog around the front of the car, grabbing Benny and her car seat. "You heard when I said we were going to the beach, right?"

"Yeah, I have a swimsuit," she answers, her voice innocent.

I scan her body. "But the pants and heels? You can't walk through sand in those."

"But…I didn't pack any other shoes."

"Listen, I'll get Benny's car seat situated. Go inside and borrow some flip-flops and a cotton sundress to wear over your bathing suit from Alma. Seriously, you'll enjoy yourself so much more if you're comfortable."

She scrunches her lips together in thought and peers down at her outfit and then back at me.

"Okay, fine." She hands me the carrier. "I'll be right back."

She turns and jogs back to the house in her four-inch heels. *Hmm...maybe, she'd be fine in her heels at the beach, after all.* I shamelessly gawk as she departs. For such a skinny thing, she has the most perfect ass.

"My baby's momma is *hot*," I sing-song to Bernadette, and she smiles, all slobbery and precious. "Yeah." I chuckle, loving the way her sweet little grins make me feel. "You know what I'm talking about."

I get the baby buckled in the back seat. My execution of the task is flawlessly precise if I say so myself. I'm kinda bummed that Cat missed it. The fact that I watched over an hour of YouTube videos on how to hook up a car seat is something I'll keep to myself.

Bernadette is fastened securely, and I steal a moment to simply take her in. Running my thumb over her wrists and the squishy rolls there brings this fierce pressure to my chest—a love that I've never felt before.

"I can't believe you're mine," I tell her. "You're perfect."

She coos, and some slobber forms at the corner of her little mouth. I swipe my thumb across her face, grabbing the spit, and wipe it on my shorts. None of which grosses me out in the least. This tiny human created this whole new version of myself—one that I didn't even know existed.

In a matter of two days, I've changed. I'm still me of course, but I'm different. Priorities have shifted, and goals have altered. I want more. So much more. And...I want it with Benny and Cat—my family.

I must make Cat see it for our future. Because it's as clear as day to me.

"She all set?" Cat asks from behind me.

Leaning in, I kiss Benny on the forehead and check her straps one more time.

I nod. "Yeah, she's perfect."

Standing from the car, I turn toward Cat. As suggested, she's in a sundress and flip-flops that Alma probably snagged from Target for twenty bucks.

"You know you are just as beautiful in that outfit as you are in your most expensive, 'fashion-y,'" I raise my hands, making air quotes with my fingers, "ones."

Her impossibly full lips tilt up into a smile. "Yeah, well, I like my 'fashion-y' clothes." She follows suit with the air quotes. "I know English is my fifth language, but I really don't think fashion-y is a word."

I open the passenger side door, motioning for Cat to step in. "You see, that's the cool thing about English. We just make shit up and call it a word." I scoff. "I do most of my work in the Starbucks downstairs. I learn new words every day."

Shutting her door, I jog around the front of the car

and get in to find Cat turned around checking Benny's car seat.

"I did it correctly." I feign hurt.

Truth is, I knew Cat would double-check. All good mothers would.

"Just checking," she says. "So what new English have come about since I've been gone over this past year?"

I pull out of the drive and head West. I'm taking the girls to a quaint little lake that has lots of shade from mature oak trees. It's part of a group of lakes in the state park a couple towns over. In my research last night, I investigated babies and beaches. Turns out children under six months of age aren't supposed to wear sunscreen, hence our trip to a little shaded beach.

Thank God for the internet. With it, I just may have a chance at being a decent father.

"Well, have you heard of sus?"

"Um, no." She giggles.

"I actually think it's losing popularity, but it means that something's suspicious."

"So people actually say, 'that's sus'?" she asks.

I huff. "Yeah, pretty much. Sounds stupid. Right? There's also 'no cap,' which means 'for real' or 'no lie.' You've heard of 'Karen?'"

"Yeah, that one started when I was still here." She shakes her head. "Poor Karen's, no? Like the women who are actually named Karen."

"Right? I'm sure they hate that one." I merge onto the

highway. "Let's see…which words have come into popularity since you've been gone? Well, there's big mad, curve, stan, shook, Gucci, slay, dead, flex, finsta, yeet, snatched, salty, sussy baka–"

She raises her hands. "Please stop. I can't. My brain can't take it." She laughs.

"I know."

"Gucci is a luxury brand…how is that slang?" she asks.

"Well, they use it like, 'it's all good, fine, or cool… it's all Gucci.'"

She turns in her seat toward me. "Is it just me, or is the population getting dumber?" she kids.

"I don't know. Somedays, I wonder." I chuckle

"It's social media, no? It's like a virus sucking our souls and our minds. I actually closed my accounts. I couldn't do it anymore. Everything is so fake, and I know that. I realize that people just show themselves how they want to be portrayed and not their reality. It was still demoralizing. Like I felt worse about myself after spending any time on there. You know? I don't think it's good. I worry about young teens, more so now that I have Benny."

"It's true. It's not healthy, for sure. Yet it's like a train wreck. You know you shouldn't—it's going to be awful—yet you watch it anyway," I say.

Her voice becomes serious. "When's the last time you said sussy baka because this might be a deal breaker for me. I mean, I have no idea what it means, but it sounds absolutely ridiculous."

I laugh. "Never. It's more of a tween video game word. I don't use most of the slang, to be honest."

"Oh, thank goodness." She leans back in her seat in dramatic fashion and swipes the top of her hand across her forehead. "Phew."

The conversation is light the rest of the way to the lake. From the moment I met Cat, even when I knew her as Daisy, it's been easy. We have a very compatible chemistry. There's never any awkward silences or weird vibes. She's fun, and we're good together.

The small sanded parking area comes into view, and I'm relieved to see only one other car, and the people beside it appear to be loading up to leave.

Although perfect and serene, the beach area is small, which could have been a problem if too many people were here. Thankfully, we'll be the only ones.

Cat unhooks Benny's car seat while I grab the bags from the truck.

"This is pretty," she says as we walk through a canopy of trees to get to the beach.

"Yeah." I agree. "I've only been here once before, but I always remembered how beautiful it was. I thought it would be ideal for Benny since the beach is in the shade."

"That's perfect," Cat exclaims as the beach comes into view.

I set up some snacks while Cat sits cross-legged on the corner of the blanket in her string bikini, nursing the baby.

Oh, fuck me.

I hold in a sigh and look up at the clouds. Why is she so insanely hot? Why must her boob always be out when I'm trying to win her over with my charm and wit…not with my sexy time skills, which…let's face it, I have in spades.

Alright, think of anything but her tit. No…breast. Ugh. Grow up, Everett.

I reach into the cooler for some snacks. We have cheese. Not sexy. Okay, good…think of cheese. There's Brie, Colby, Muenster, provolone, Feta, blue cheese, mozzarella, cheddar–"

"Are you okay over there?" Cat chuckles. "What are you whispering about?"

I shake my head. "Nothing. Just cheese."

Smooth.

"Would you like me to make you a plate of snacks while you feed her?"

She shakes her head. "I'm not really hungry right now, but I'd love something to drink."

I unzip the beverage cooler. "I can do that. I have wine, beer, pop, water, and sparkling water. I wasn't sure what you'd want."

"A sparkling water would be great." She smiles.

I hand her the glass bottle.

"It's such a beautiful day," she says before she takes a sip of water.

"Yeah, it is."

I remove my shoes and shirt, leaving me in just my swim trunks, and I take a seat on the blanket. My legs are stretched out before me as I face the water.

From my peripheral, I can see Cat checking me out, and I can't pretend it doesn't make me feel good.

The blue lake water bobs with soft waves, the crest of each sparkle with the sun's reflection creating a moving diamond painting. It's stunning against the tree lined horizon of deep green and the bright blue sky full of soft clouds.

I can't remember the last time I stopped to take in my surroundings like this. Life is one big string of busy moments—work, friends, parties, and more work. Sitting here with Cat calms me and drowns out the noise of my life. It's refreshing.

Cat finishes nursing and burping Benny before she sets her down in the infant car seat.

"Asleep again? All babies seem to do is eat and sleep." I grin.

"At this age, yes…unless it's nighttime, and then she'll want to be wide awake for hours, just for fun." She shakes her head.

"Do you want to swim?" I ask, and Cat shoots her eyes at Benny. "She's asleep. No one else is here. If anyone shows up, we'll see them coming down the path long before they reach the beach, and we'll swim back."

She chews on her bottom lip. "Okay. Yeah, we'll hear her if she wakes."

"Definitely, and the water gets chest deep quickly. So we'll only be fifteen or so feet out, close enough to see her, too."

She nods. "You're right, and it's so beautiful. It'd be a shame not to."

"Exactly." I stand and extend my hand to Cat.

She takes it, and I pull her up.

The water is warm yet still refreshing. It's clear and clean… a little piece of heaven.

"I loved living in Michigan," Cat says when we stop walking once the water reaches chest-deep. "It's so beautiful here, the lakes and seasons, especially."

"Yeah, it is. You know, everyone loves autumn, and I get it the foliage is gorgeous. But summer is where it's at."

"I love all the seasons," Cat says before dipping her head under the water. She surfaces and wipes her hair back. "Winter gets a bad rap, but snow is beautiful, and I love skiing."

I chuckle. "I've never been. It's kind of a wealthy person's pastime. Growing up, Mom never had money to buy me all the ski gear and take me. As an adult, I've just never gone."

Cat's cheeks redden. "I'm sorry. Was that a snobby thing to say? *I love skiing.*"

"Of course not." I reach across the water and squeeze her arm in reassurance. "If you're in Michigan, in the winter, we'll have to go…you can teach me."

She smiles. "That'd be fun."

Cat leans back and floats atop the water, taking in the sky above.

We swim, and splash, and constantly look toward the shore where Benny sleeps peacefully.

It's fun…and so very hot. I throb with desire for the literal goddess before me. I want her so much it's painful. She's stunning and simply irresistible. But today's not about that. I've had that.

God, I've had that.

Memories from the casino rush back, and my need grows.

No.

I blow out a breath. I want more. Today is about discovering *more.* Keeping the memories with Cat locked up in my highlight reel isn't enough. Not when I could have her in real life and for more than a day. I can't blow it.

"What are you thinking?" She swims toward me. The water bobs against her lips, making them wet and more inviting.

I clear my throat. "Nothing."

She plays with my hands under the water, threading her fingers through mine.

What is she doing?

She shakes her head. "No, you're thinking about something. You get this look."

"I get a look?"

"Yeah, when you want to say something but you're holding back. Your face looks a certain way, like back on the beach with the cooler and the cheese."

I sigh. "I just want us to have a great day."

"And?" She quirks a brow.

I press my lips together and pull in a deep breath through my nose. "And..." I swallow hard. "I want to touch you."

She surprises me by asking, "Where do you want to touch me?"

"Everywhere."

She stands and steps toward me, so our wet bodies are a mere breath apart. "I want that, too," she whispers against my lips.

Holy hell.

I splay my hands across her tight belly. Her chest rises, and she sucks in a breath. She pulls her bottom lip into her mouth, and the sight almost causes me to come undone like a teen boy watching porn for the first time.

Caterina owns me.

"Everywhere?" I question.

She takes a quick glance at the deserted beach and sleeping baby, then turns back to me. "Everywhere."

With that invitation, I lower my hand into her bikini bottoms and slip a finger into her warmth. We groan in unison.

Leaning in, I kiss her collarbone and up her neck as my finger moves inside her. My thumb pays special attention to the bundle of nerves that needs the most attention.

"Everett…" she cries as she starts to ride my hand. My name, my real name, falling from her lips as she chases her release is the sexiest thing I've ever heard in my life.

I pump my hand harder, rubbing her front wall, desperate for her to fall over the edge and into my arms. She claws at my chest, her eyes closed as she starts to whimper and move faster. She's so close.

Cat, wet and shaking in this deserted lake has me more turned on than I've ever been. She's going to fall, and then I'm going to bury myself so deep inside her that she'll never want me to stop.

"Oh, my God, Everett…I'm…ahhhh…" she cries as she shakes against me. Her head falls against my chest, and her hot breath gives me goose bumps.

My fingers continue their assault until she's ridden out her orgasm and slumps against me.

I remove my hand from the tiny piece of fabric and cradle her face between my hands. She's so amazingly beautiful. I want her. God, I need her. She needs me, too. I see it in her eyes.

My gaze falls from her green eyes to her lips and back again. She drops her stare to my lips and closes her eyes. I breathe in, close my eyes, and lean forward.

A shrill little cry from a pair of tiny lungs sounds right before my lips touch hers.

Dammit.

Cat bolts back and looks at the shore and back at me. The lust immediately vanishes from her gaze that now holds doubt and confusion. Within a second, she's turned to swim toward the shore, leaving me horny as hell and alone in the lake.

I'm not sure how I saw that going, but I didn't see it ending like this.

I need a few minutes for my arousal to calm down before I head to shore.

Okay, non-sexy thoughts…

Cheddar. Gouda. Swiss. Provolone. Feta…

CHAPTER 12

CAT

*L*ove is running through the sprinkler in Alma's backyard with Alma's mother, known to Love as Gigi. Alma's mother was a neglectful mother who was addicted to drugs for most of Alma's life, so it's amazing to see her now as such an attentive grandma.

True success stories are so rare when it comes to addiction, so each one I see brings me so much joy. It may have taken Lee-Anne, Alma's mother, a good twenty-five years, but she did it, and I'm so happy for her. I pray she never goes back. While one never knows if someone will relapse, I feel in my heart that Lee-Anne won't. The death of her husband changed her. She's not the same person, and I don't think she ever wants to be.

"Your mom looks so happy," I say to Alma who is sitting in a lounge chair on the deck beside me.

Her husband Amos is overseeing everything at *The Lair*, a nonprofit organization they run that helps troubled youth, so she could spend the day with me.

"I know. It's been years, and I still have to pinch myself. I wish I'd always had her this way, but I'm just so happy to have a sober mother now, especially for Love's sake."

"She really is a great grandma," I say.

Benny sleeps against my chest, and I gently tap her back.

"She is." Alma agrees. "How are your parents doing with the whole grandparent's role?"

A smile comes to my face thinking of my parents. "Great. Oh, they are in love with Benny. So doting and affectionate. This girl will not go a minute in this life without knowing she's adored."

"That's great." Alma smiles. "Every child deserves that. I'm so happy for you, Cat. You seem happier than you've ever been."

"I am," I say truthfully. "Becoming a mother changed me and my priorities. You know? I only do the things that bring me joy. I don't have time to waste. Minutes are precious, and they fly by."

Alma looks at her daughter. "They sure do. It goes so

fast." She turns her gaze to Benny. "I love every age. I remember when Love was that small. I wanted to keep her that tiny and precious forever. But each age brings something incredible, and I've loved every one. Right now, Love's learning about the world around her so quickly. She's starting to think about the bigger picture. You know…right and wrong, and why. She questions everything and wants to understand. And, at the same time, she's still so young and innocent. It's fun to watch her mind work."

"She's a good kid," I tell my friend.

"Thank you. I think so." Alma smiles. "Benny will be great, too, because she has you."

"I hope so." I kiss my sleeping baby's soft head.

"You've been awfully quiet about your date yesterday." She raises a brow.

I lean my head back against the lounge chair. "Ugh, I know."

"Well, I'm all ears."

"I'm embarrassed."

"Why?" Alma chuckles.

"Well…I made a big deal about wanting to get to know Everett as a person outside of our days as Bernard and Daisy. I want to know the real Everett, the father of my daughter."

"Right, all good. So where does the embarrassing part come to play?" Alma inquires.

I describe the setting of the picturesque lake. "It was

just the two of us in the water. He was so hot. I mean… the guy is gorgeous. There was an attraction and emotions. And it's been so long…" I cover my face.

"You did it in the water?" Alma giggles.

"No." I huff. "Not quite. It probably would've gotten there if Benny hadn't woken up. But he did make me orgasm with his hand, and it was amazing. The guy has skills."

"There's nothing wrong with that," Alma reassures me. "You obviously have a deep attraction based on your day together before you flew to Moscow. And that day led to a baby. So of course you're going to have lust when it comes to Everett."

"That's the thing, though. I know we are compatible in bed, but I can't let my brain be clouded by that. Love is so much more than sex. It scares me, if I'm honest, because I'm so attracted to him that I'm afraid it's blinding me to everything else. The truth is, I hardly know him. He's my daughter's father, and he wants to be in her life, and I don't *know* him. Then when I'm with him, all I want to do is have sex. It's an issue." I groan.

Alma smiles, pressing her lips together as if she's holding in a laugh. "I think you have to let go a little bit, Cat. You've had three great days with him, starting with the epic day at the casino. So far there are no red flags. As I said, I don't know him well, but from what I've seen and heard, he's a really cool guy. He's trying hard to get to know you and spend time with Benny. It's okay to be attracted to him and get to know him on a deeper level at the same time. They're not mutually exclusive. You can do both."

"I can't risk letting go," I say. "I'm a mother now. I must do what's right. You understand that. When he touches me, I lose all ability to think straight. I know myself, and I can't do both. I won't chance making another mistake now that I have to worry about more than just myself. I was in a miserable marriage for ten years. I'd rather my daughter be raised by a single, happy mother than by two unhappy parents."

Alma reaches out and grabs my hand before squeezing it. "I understand that completely. You of all people deserve to find your soul mate, and maybe it's not Everett. But you won't know if you don't give him a chance."

I release a dry chuckle. "Not everyone gets a soul mate."

"Maybe not, but you will. I know it."

"I hope you're right," I say with a sad smile.

Alma winks. "I know I am. Mark my words, Caterina Avilova Araya, you will find your soul mate because I don't live in a world where someone as kind and wonderful as you doesn't have one."

Alma releases my hand and looks off into the distance. I know this look well, and over the years, it's changed from complete desperation to a fond remembrance.

Finally, she shrugs, giving voice to her thoughts. "I've had two, and I've been given two…your one is out there."

I think of Leo, Alma's first husband and my former brother-in-law. He was such a bright light in my life, the one who for many years kept me sane. Before Alma, he was my one true piece of family here, even more so than his brother, my ex-husband. I miss Leo. Everyday.

"I'd like to visit Leo today before Everett picks us up, if that's okay. I don't want to get busy and run out of time to visit his grave while I'm here."

"Oh, absolutely. We can head down to the farmers' market and pick up some flowers before we go. One of Love's favorite things is picking out flowers for her daddy in heaven. We haven't been in a while, so we're due a visit, too. What time is Everett coming?"

"He's going to get us for dinner around six," I state.

"Great. That leaves plenty of time." She looks up at the sky. "Plus, it's what Love and I like to call heaven skies today."

"What's that?"

"See how perfect the sky is? The blue is vibrant. The clouds are bright white and so fluffy that it looks like you could jump in them, and they'd wrap around you like a soft pile of fluff. Then and this is the most important part, see how the sun's rays shine through the clouds in brilliant strands of light that look like they're being sent from heaven? The combination of all of that…looks like heaven, doesn't it?"

"It does look like heaven," I agree with a smile as I take in the sky.

"Heaven skies." Alma grins. "And on days with heaven skies, Leo can hear us better."

"Perfect," I say.

Alma stands from the lounge chair. "I'm going to get Love dried off and changed. Then we can go."

She takes off down the deck steps.

I turn my attention back toward the sky. It is beautiful today. Maybe Leo will hear me and send me a sign because God knows, I don't know what I'm doing with Everett. I need clarity.

Leaning in, I kiss Benny's soft head and breathe her in.

My head is spinning with a hundred questions, doubts, and scenarios. Yet there's one thought that rings true. Whatever happens—Benny is my number one. Whatever decisions I make will be for her.

I won't mess it up.

CHAPTER 13

EVERETT

I tighten my grasp on the steering wheel. It's different with Cat today. The dynamic is… weird. We haven't said more than a few pleasantries to each other, and I hate it.

Yesterday, she rode my hand until she screamed. And today…silence.

No, this won't do.

"What'd my girls do today?" I force my voice to sound as chill as possible, and I think it does. There's no sign of internal panic in my words.

Cat looks out the window. "Alma took the day off work, and we just hung out with her daughter, Love, and Alma's mother."

"So lots of girl talk?" I ask.

"Basically." I can hear the grin in her voice.

"And what does she think about our situation?"

From what I gather, Alma is the most important person Cat has in the States. She's staying with her and definitely talks about her and her family the most. I've met Alma several times through Quinn, Cassie, and Tannon, and though we're not close, I hope I've made a good impression. Alma barely knows me, yet I have a feeling that her opinion means everything to Cat.

She turns to me, and I take my eyes from the road for just a moment to take her in. She's fresh-faced today, wearing nothing but a dab of mascara. She looks young and sweet, and so insanely beautiful. Her olive skin tone brings out her green irises, somehow causing them to shine brighter.

She's so gorgeous she almost doesn't appear real, like she's walking around with her own personal goddess filter. The crazy thing is, as far as I can tell, she's just as perfect on the inside. Besides her choice of residing countries, I haven't found a flaw in her. I can't really fault her for moving home to be close to her family, either. Though in an ideal world, her parents would live in Ann Arbor.

"She said I should keep an open mind," she states.

"An open mind about?"

"Us…You…Our situation."

Pressing my lips together, I grin. "Okay. I think that

sounds like sound advice. An open mind is…good." I knew I liked Alma.

"Yeah, it is…but…" She sighs.

I groan. "No buts, just an open mind."

"I think we should talk about yesterday. Make some ground rules."

I'm silent, allowing her to continue, but I'm already bummed because I know where this conversation is going.

Her voice is unnaturally steady. "It's obvious that you and I have chemistry. That's never been in question, no? I mean, from the very beginning—a year ago—that was clear. But it's different now. This isn't just for fun. This is about her." She nods toward the back seat where Benny sleeps in her car seat. "We need to find our way as parents and…whatever else we're going to be together. I have less than two weeks here, and it's important that we learn more about each other and you learn about us. Ugh…" she sighs. "I'm blabbing. Am I making any sense?"

"You're making complete sense," I answer, though it pains me to do so. "You're saying that we should cut out the spicy times because we have that down. We need to focus on the getting to know each other part, without the hormonal distractions."

"Yes!" she agrees far too enthusiastically for my liking.

I can't help but laugh. "Don't sound so excited about the fact that you don't want me to touch you anymore."

"It's not about wanting or not wanting it. We both know you're really good at it."

"Oh yeah?" I raise a brow.

"Stop." She playfully hits my arm. "Of course, you are. We have no problems in that area, and that's why we need to avoid it altogether. Being together like that will only muddle everything else. We should be spending this time learning about one another. If life was spent in bed, then maybe it wouldn't matter."

"I could definitely spend my life in bed with you," I offer.

"Be serious." She chuckles. "There's more to a relationship than sex, and if that's really what you want…a relationship—"

I cut her off. "It is."

"Then we need to figure out the rest without the distraction," she answers.

I remove my hands from the steering wheel briefly, holding them up in the surrender position. "Okay, you win. We'll get to know each other." I return my grasp to the wheel.

"That means no kissing," she says.

"I know."

"And nothing below the clothes."

"I know."

"No touching with your hands or lips anywhere on my body." She smirks.

"Got it. Don't make you feel good. Check." My pointer finger makes a check mark in the air.

She chuckles. "The key to a good relationship is being able to make each other feel good in other ways."

I nod. "Gotcha. I see what you're saying. Challenge accepted."

"Alright, so we're good."

"We're definitely good, Cat." I shoot her a grin. "So what else did you and Alma talk about today?"

"You know. The normal stuff—life, family, job…and you. We did go into the farmers' market in town and get some flowers to put on Leo's grave."

"Leo is…?"

"My brother-in-law, Alma's first husband. He was incredible, and the brother I never had. In most ways, he was kinder to me than Stephen, my ex, ever was. I don't know what I would've done without him during my first few years here."

"I'm glad you had him," I say.

"Me too."

"I've heard others talk about him over the years. He seemed like an awesome guy."

"He was…one of the best." She clears her throat and changes the subject. "So what are we doing today. We've been driving for a while."

"Ah." I nod. "So it seems we were on the same wavelength about getting to know each other better because we are having dinner at my mom's."

"Really? Oh, good. I can't wait to meet her."

"She can't wait to meet you either or Benny. She's so excited to be a grandma. You have no idea." I smile, thinking back to my mother's shriek over the phone when I told her.

"Where does she live?" Cat asks.

"In Wayne, outside of Detroit…kind of by the airport." There's a dip in my voice. "It's not the best neighborhood, but she likes it. She won't move no matter how much I ask her to. I've offered to get her an apartment in Ann Arbor, but she won't take my help. Actually, there are some things you should probably know since we're getting to know each other on a deeper level and all."

My heart beats rapidly within my chest at the thought of talking about my childhood, and I hate that it does. I'm not ashamed of my upbringing or my mother, but to an outsider looking in, I realize it doesn't look great.

Cat reaches over and squeezes my thigh. "It's okay, Everett. You know I'm not going to judge you." She must sense my hesitation.

"First, it's important for you to know that my mother is a good person. She's kind and loving."

"I believe it. You're the same way, so there's no doubt in my mind that you were loved."

I smile, adoring the fact that Cat sees the good in everything.

"So my dad left us when I was a baby. I don't have one memory of him. The memories I do have are of my mother chasing men, trying to get someone to love her." I scoff. "Complete losers, all of them. She raised me on her own. She worked multiple jobs to make sure I had everything I needed. I was never without food or clothes. She tried her best. But she was so desperate to be loved by a man. She made stupid decisions all the time, like giving her credit card to a jerk that she thought she was going to marry. He charged that thing up and left her. It took years for her to pay it off. It was always something like that. She'd fall in love with a total lowlife. He'd use her for a while, take what he could, and then leave. Every time."

I swallow hard, shaking my head with a sad laugh. "I made it my mission to make her laugh and feel loved so that she'd forget about the revolving door of heartbreak she was perpetually stuck in. But I was never enough, and the life we had, wasn't either. She was sad and lonely...all the time."

"I'm so sorry," Cat says. "I can't imagine how hard that had to be."

"It sucked," I admit. "I'm not going to lie and tell you it hasn't affected my adult life. I haven't been in a genuine long-term relationship ever. Watching a woman I adore be so blinded by the pursuit of love for so long that she couldn't see her own worth left a really negative taste in my mouth. You know?"

Cat nods. "Yeah."

"However, I also know that it all started when my father abandoned us. Growing up without a dad was just as hard, and I swore I'd never leave my child. That's the thing about being an adult, I'm not a child without options anymore, I can be better. I can avoid the mistakes of my parents. I'm committed to you and Benny. I want to be a great father. I want her to know that I will always be there for her. If you choose to believe anything I say regarding us, please believe that."

She squeezes my thigh again. "I do, Everett. I know you'll be there for Benny. I believe you."

I smile. "Okay, good."

CHAPTER 14

CAT

It's not the worst neighborhood I've seen, but it's definitely not the best. It's nowhere I'd choose to live.

"You lived here growing up?" I ask Everett as I unclick Benny's car seat carrier.

"No, not this building but others like it. We moved around a lot," he answers.

He offers to hold Benny's carrier, and I hand it over.

"Are you ready to meet your grandma?" he asks Benny as she stirs awake.

I follow Everett up the stairs to the third floor of the apartment building. I'm careful not to touch the metal railing as we ascend, as a clumpy yellowish substance was dripping from the railing on the first floor. Someone has spray painted the word *bitch* about fifty times on the stairwell walls in black paint.

Cozy and welcoming, I think, careful to keep my face emotionless. I know it took a lot for Everett to bring me here and open up to me about his childhood. I don't want to seem judgmental.

I let out a sigh of relief when Everett stops before an apartment door, inserts a key, and opens it.

"Mom, we're here," he calls as he steps into the apartment.

The small space is the complete opposite of the stairwell. It's comfortable and inviting. The furniture is mismatched but clean. A small end table between the floral sofa and orange oversized rocking chair has a flickering blue candle making the room smell summery. I'd bet the candle's name is something close to *Summer Waves*.

An older, female version of Everett hurries toward us with a large smile on her face. She's beautiful, her sandy blond hair wrapped up in a scrunchie bun atop her head. She has the same big hazel eyes as Everett and an identical smile to his as well. Yet though stunning, she also wears the skin of someone who's had a hard life.

"Hi! You must be the beautiful Caterina I've heard so much about!" She pulls me into a hug. "It's so nice to meet you."

"You too," I say.

"You can call me Sarah or Mom or Grandma. Whatever you want!" She looks over her shoulder at the candle. "I only have it lit because I know the baby is too young to move or grab it."

"Oh, it's fine," I say. "It smells good. Like summer."

She grins wide. "Yes, it's called *Beach Walk*." She hugs Everett, and then looks at Benny, covering her mouth with her hands. "She's gorgeous." Her eyes fill with tears.

"I told ya." Everett smiles proudly at Benny.

It's true. The two of us made an adorable human.

"I just can't believe it," she exclaims. Turning to me, she shakes her head. "I was so shocked when my Everett told me he was a dad. It's wonderful news. I hear you two don't know each other well, but let me tell you…my boy is going to be an incredible father."

"I know he is," I reassure her.

"Can I hold her?" She looks back and forth between Everett and me.

"Of course," I say.

Everett leads the way to the floral sofa that looks like it's straight out of the 1980s, sets down Benny's carrier, and starts unbuckling her.

He hands Benny to his mother, and her eyes widen in wonder. "Oh, she is perfect. Is she a good baby?"

I find her question amusing only because I never realized how many people ask this of new mothers. I've lost count of how many people have asked me if Benny *is a good baby*. Like are their bad babies out there robbing convenience stores? It's a perplexing question.

My answer is always the same. "She's the best."

"Oh, good. Everett was a great baby, too. He slept well and didn't fuss. As long as he was fed and had a dry diaper, he was fine. He wasn't a spoiled baby."

Another idea I can't get on board with is spoiling an infant. It's not possible. I've had many people tell me to be careful not to spoil her. *Don't hold her too much* is the most common advice given, to which I ignore. I hold her as much as humanly possible.

Sarah continues to ooh and aah over Bernadette and tells stories from when Everett was this age. She speaks of the memories with such fondness even though I know it must have been a very lonely time for her.

She asks about my life in Moscow and my parents. Our conversations are all very pleasant, and I can tell she's a good person.

After a while, Benny starts to fuss. "You think she's hungry?" Sarah asks.

I nod. "Yeah, it's about that time."

She hands over the baby and stands from the sofa. "While you feed her, I'll get dinner on the table. I made one of Everett's favorites."

Everett follows her to the kitchen area.

I nurse Benny and listen to the two of them chatting away. They seem to have such a great relationship, and that makes me happy. I think the way a man treats his mother is a good indication of how he'd treat a wife.

Stephen treated his mother with indifference. There was no true affection there…much like our marriage.

After I've burped and changed Benny's diaper, I set her down in the car seat carrier. Her eyes are droopy, and I know she'll doze off. I run my finger along her soft cheek and kiss her head. "Love you, mi amor."

I leave Benny to nap and join Everett and his mother at the small, round table pushed against the corner of the kitchen area.

"Just in time," Sarah says. "Everything's ready." She gets up from the table. Sliding her hands into some gloved potholders, she opens the oven and pulls out a casserole dish.

She brings it over to the table and places it on a dish towel in the center. I'm not sure exactly what she's prepared. The dish bubbles around the edges, and Sarah plops a large serving spoon in the mystery concoction.

"I made one of Everett's favorite meals, chicken and rice. We ate this at least once a week growing up," she adds proudly.

"Mom. I told you, Cat doesn't eat meat." He shoots an apologetic look my way.

"Oh, no. I forgot. I'm so sorry," Sarah says.

I shake my head and wave a hand through the air. "It's fine. I love rice. Not a problem."

"Are you sure?" she asks. "I'm sure I can find something else."

I take a seat in one of the chairs and scoot up to the table. "I'm positive. Don't even worry about it."

Sarah nods and exchanges a look with Everett before the two of them join me at the table. She plops a large scoop of the meal onto each of our plates.

As a plant-based eater living in a meat eater's world, I'm very used to situations like this. But, honestly, it's usually not a problem. There's always something else…a dish of green beans, rolls, or a side salad that I can munch on. There's literally only white rice in a gravy with chunks of chicken on my plate. It's a very colorless meal without many options.

"Thanks, Mom. It looks great." Everett says.

"It's very easy to make," Sarah says to me. "Just need a box of instant rice, four cans of cream of chicken soup, and some chicken breasts. Cube the chicken and place it all together in a casserole dish with a little water, and it cooks up perfectly. Plus, it's not only easy but inexpensive. When Everett was a boy, I'd wait for the chicken to go on sale and snatch some up. I could make a huge dish of the stuff for a few bucks, and it would last us a couple of meals."

"Oh, well, that's a bonus." I smile.

"Yeah, single moms are always looking for ways to save. Right?" she asks.

"Of course." Using my fork, I scrape some of the

casserole to a new location on my plate. Another technique I've mastered over the years is moving food so it looks like it's been eaten without having to actually eat it. A skill I probably learned from a toddler. But it works.

I don't like hurting people's feelings or offending them, and in my experience, people are oddly attached to their meat dishes. So mastering food manipulation is a must.

"It's delicious, Mom," Everett says.

When Sarah turns to Everett, I place an empty fork in my mouth and pull it out with a, "Mmm, very good."

I really am a toddler.

"I'm glad you like it." She smiles. "You know, I prefer cream of chicken, but really any cream soup will work—cream of mushroom, celery, potato. So there are options to vegan it up if you want."

"Great." I force a grin.

Condensed creamed soups are something I've never really understood, but many Americans love to cook with them. I understand that Sarah did what she had to do to feed her son. But Stephen's parents loved dishes made with them, especially around Thanksgiving, and they're millionaires. I don't get it.

Besides the actual meal, dinner is wonderful. We're engrossed in conversation and laughter—so much so that Sarah doesn't notice how little I eat.

Benny starts to fuss, and Sarah asks if she can

get her.

"Sure," I say. "I'll clear the table."

Everett's mother scurries off toward Benny while Everett helps me clean up the kitchen.

"I'm sorry," he whispers.

I shake my head. "Don't be. It was great."

"We'll stop somewhere on the way home to pick up some food," he says, placing a plate in the dishwasher.

"I'm fine, really. I loved all the stories from when you were a kid." I grin, looking over at my handsome baby daddy.

He chuckles. "She has a crazy good memory. Doesn't she?"

"She does." I hand him the plastic glasses from the table. "I'm so glad I got to meet her. We must take lots of pictures before we leave. Who knows how big Benny will be the next time she sees her?"

My statement causes a frown to form on Everett's face, but he quickly turns his mouth up into a grin. "We definitely will."

After a few more tales of young Everett, lots of pictures, and promises to visit again, we're back in the car and on our return trip to Ann Arbor.

Tonight was wonderful, and I'm so happy that I got to meet Everett's mother and that she got to meet her granddaughter. If anything, it cemented the fact that Benny will always have family here in Michigan—good people who love her. It's not going to be ideal figuring out custody and visitation between the two continents, but it's important for her to know her dad and his side of the family. A child can never have too much love.

Yet listening to Sarah's stories and knowing what I know about her past—I feel sorry for her. I know what it's like to want love so badly and have it be out of reach. I fought for ten years to make my marriage what I thought it'd be when I said, "I do."

I held out for the happily ever after, knowing it would always be out of reach. Sarah's story is mine with different details. And look how it affected her son. He's spent his life trying to make her happy. He grew up seeking out women to save.

That's how he found me, isn't it?

I was alone, sad, and heartbroken at that casino bar, and Everett was drawn to me like a moth to a flame. His knight in shining armor radar buzzing loudly at the sight of me nursing my martini at the peak of my grief.

If there's anything that I want to teach my daughter, it's that she doesn't need a man to rescue her. She has everything she needs to save herself. Children don't learn through lectures; they imitate what they see. The greatest gift I can give Bernadette is a strong, confident mother who is truly happy—all on my own. I'll create a life fit for us queens and choose joy every day.

I won't settle or chase love.

I'll show her that I am enough, and therefore, she'll believe that she is, too.

CHAPTER 15

EVERETT

"It's okay. It's okay." I hold Benny in my arms, rocking her back and forth as she screams.

Two hours.

Who knew that two hours would feel like an eternity when Cat dropped the baby off? "I'll be back in two hours," she said. "She'll sleep most of it."

Well, Benny's not sleeping. In fact, she's the opposite of sleeping. She's screaming.

"What do I do?" I beg Asher for help.

He shrugs. "I don't know anything about babies. You're the one spending every second online learning about them. If anyone here"—he circles his arm around our apartment—"knows what to do, it's you."

I groan, throwing my head back as I continue to bounce Benny in my arms. "But. I don't. I begged Cat to leave her with me, and now she's never going to trust me with her again."

"It's not your fault she's crying," he shouts so I can hear him over the screams.

I shake my head. "I'm sure it will be."

Cat and Alma went over to Quinn and Ollie's house to decorate it or some shit. They want to surprise the newlyweds when they get back from their honeymoon in a few days. Cat wanted to take the baby with her, but I insisted on watching her. Bonding time and all that.

This was all my idea.

Now, look at me. I'm losing my mind with a baby who screams entirely too loud for her size. How big are her lungs? This is my first time watching her on my own, and although I'm no expert—I'd classify this as a big fat failure.

Is Cat going to read into this? Of course, she will.

These two weeks are supposed to be time for us to get to know each other and to bond as a family. She leaves our child alone with me, against her better judgment, and Benny literally falls apart. How will Cat not think this is a sign? I'm not positive what it will mean to her, but it will signify something. My lack of fathering ability will be front and center, I'm sure.

"Did you check her diaper?" Asher paces back and forth across the living room, his hands at his sides.

"Yes. Dry."

"She hungry?"

I shrug. "I don't know. Cat fed her right before she left. She told me that she could go two hours without eating easily. It's just been two hours now. Did you call Tannon?" I ask; my question is desperate. Our bestie has a little boy a few months older than Benny. Surely, she's our best bet at figuring this out.

"Voicemail. I called and texted. Nothing."

"What about Cassie?" I plead.

"She doesn't know about babies." He furrows his brow. "Plus, she's working."

I hold Benny against my shoulder and gently pat her back. The scream is so much worse this close to my ear.

"I don't care. Text her to come up. Tell her it's an emergency. She's a girl. Maybe she has a sixth sense about these things."

Asher scoffs and pulls his phone from his back pocket. "Okay."

Thankfully Cassie works downstairs at the Starbucks below our apartment. She rushes into the apartment a minute later.

"What's the emergency? I left Henry to man the place by himself, and you know that won't go well." she gasps for breath, her hand splayed across the fabric of her green work apron. She must've run up the steps as quickly as she could. I adore her.

"The baby won't stop crying," I say.

She steps toward me and asks all the normal questions that I've already covered with Asher a hundred times.

"Let me see her." She holds out her arms.

I hand my daughter over.

She presses her hand against Benny's forehead. "Oh my gosh, she's burning up, E."

"I just thought she was hot from getting herself all worked up from crying," I say.

Cassie shakes her head. "No, this is a definite fever. I don't know much about babies, but I know fevers are bad news. They can be serious, and she feels really hot. I think you should take her in."

"To the hospital?" My eyes widen.

"Yeah. You don't want to risk it," she says.

"Okay, thank you. I'm going." I take Benny back and strap her into the car seat carrier. "Ash, can you drive?"

He nods. "Yeah, sure."

I snatch up Benny's diaper bag and carrier and rush outside. Pulling my phone out, I text Cat to let her know what's going on and ask her to meet me at the hospital.

I'm panicked and have so many emotions swirling around my mind. I pray it's nothing serious. I no longer care that Cat will probably hate me and be disappointed that I didn't keep Benny safe. I only care about the health of my daughter.

"To Mott's?" Asher asks from the driver's seat.

"Shh." I rub my thumb over Benny's hand, trying to calm her. "Yeah, Mott's," I respond from the back seat.

The University of Michigan's Mott's Children's Hospital is one of the best in the world—and thankfully, it's less than a five-minute drive from our apartment.

Asher pulls up to the emergency door entrance, and I grab Benny and rush out.

I don't think I'm speaking in coherent sentences as I tell the nurse at the registration desk what's wrong. But she must gather the main details because she leads us back to a room. Her warm smile calms my racing heart just a tad. Surely, she wouldn't be smiling if something was gravely wrong with Benny. Right?

The doctor doesn't make us wait long, and the second she takes Benny from me, a sense of relief, albeit minor, washes over me. This is a world-class doctor. Benny's in good hands…way better hands than my own.

She's going to be okay.

Please.

She has to be…

* * *

MY DAUGHTER SLEEPS against my chest, and I hold her tight. I press my lips against her soft hair and breathe in. She smells like baby shampoo, and it's one of the best scents in the world. How has no one ever told me how amazing baby shampoo smells?

The exam room door flies open, and a wide-eyed Cat rushes in.

"I got here as soon as I could. I didn't hear my phone go off. I just got your text a few minutes ago. What's wrong? Is she okay?" Tears fall down her cheeks.

"She's fine." I sigh. "She has an ear infection. The doctor said they're very common. They gave her some Motrin and her first dose of antibiotics. She'll be good as new in no time."

"An ear infection?" Cat clarifies.

"Yeah."

"Okay." She nods, processing the information.

"The doctor said that they're caused by a bacteria that gets in the ear. Very common in babies and easily treatable. The antibiotics will clear it up, and she'll start feeling better soon." I kiss Benny's head. "I swear, minutes after they gave her the pain meds, she fell right to sleep."

"I want to speak to the doctor." Cat swipes her hand across her cheek, wiping her tears, and sits in the chair beside me.

"Of course. She's getting our discharge paperwork ready. I can let her know you're here." I hand Benny over to Cat, and she holds her against her chest, kissing her head.

"I'm sorry," I say. "She wouldn't stop crying and had a fever, so I rushed her here. I didn't know what to do, but

I didn't want to take any chances. I'm sorry if I scared you."

She extends an arm toward me, and I take her hand in mine. "No, you did the right thing. Better safe than sorry. She's never been sick before. I was just worried."

"So you're not mad at me?"

She quirks a brow. "Why would I be mad at you?"

"I don't know. She got sick on my watch." I squeeze her hand again before letting it go.

She smiles. "You didn't give her an ear infection, Everett. Babies get sick. It was bound to happen. It's definitely not your fault."

"Okay." I let out a sigh of relief.

"Oh, my gosh." She presses her lips together. "You were really worried."

"Well, yeah," I say. "I want to show you that I can be a good dad. You're such a great mom."

She dips her chin, taking in our sleeping angel with a grin, before looking back up at me. "I know I'm protective of her, Everett. I can't help it. But I've also had more time adjusting to the idea of parenthood. You've had a week. I wasn't mother of the year on day one. There's a learning curve." She chuckles.

I shake my head. "No, I bet you were perfect from the start."

"I can assure you I wasn't. No one is. I'm not spending time with you to rate your parenting skills or anything. I can already tell you'll be a great dad because you want to be. I simply wanted to make sure that you're a good person, which you are. And...I wanted to know that you wanted Benny in your life, which you do. The rest will come."

"So I passed?" I raise a brow.

"There was no test." She grins.

"But if there was?" I smirk.

"You'd pass."

"Yes! Awesome. Okay." I do a random victory dance, which causes Cat to laugh.

She's beautiful always, even when she cries. But her laughter is something I'm quickly becoming addicted to. I'd do just about anything to hear it.

"So I'm going to go get the doctor," I say.

"Okay."

"And then we'll hang out?"

"Okay." She grins.

"And...just to be clear, I passed?"

She chuckles and shoos me away. "Just go."

I raise my hands in surrender. "Going."

CHAPTER 16

CAT

*E*verett sets out the containers of food on the blanket. He's prepared a picnic for Benny and me, and it's really sweet. Adorable even.

It's straight out of a romance novel, complete with a patchwork quilt, a picturesque park, and a fabric-lined wicker basket.

"I can't believe you've never had their food," Everett says of the restaurant where he ordered the takeout. "I mean, eighty percent of the menu is vegetarian."

Screwing off the cap of a water bottle, I take a sip. "I love Mediterranean food. I just didn't order it much when I lived here for some reason. I guess I didn't know many good restaurants."

He hands me a plate. "Well, prepare to have your mind blown."

"Really?" I laugh. "That good?"

"Yes, that good." He scoffs. "If they can win me over, a burger and fries kind of guy, you'll be amazed."

He pops open the lid to the containers. "So I got you two salads, tabbouleh and fattoush. There's warm pita bread for both. Both are really good, but I'm partial to the tabbouleh."

"I love tabbouleh," I say.

"Yeah?"

"Definitely. I actually make this myself, though I'm not sure my recipe is mind-blowing." I shoot him a wink.

I scoop each of the salads onto my plate and take a bite of the tabbouleh.

"Oh, that's good," I say through a mouthful. The flavors of the parsley, onions, tomatoes, and lemon juice pop in my mouth. "You can tell they use a really good olive oil. That's key."

"You can tell the difference between olive oils?" he questions.

"Of course. Olive oil can make or break a meal."

"It all tastes the same to me." He takes a large bite of the salad.

I shake my head. "No way. There's a clear difference between quality oil and the cheap stuff."

"If you say so." He chuckles. "Here, try this, but you

need to eat it with a bite of pita." He plops a spoonful of what I know to be baba ganouj on my plate. "I spent my whole life thinking I hated eggplant, but this changed my mind."

I scoop up a bite of the eggplant onto the flatbread and take a bite. My eyes roll back, and I groan.

"Right?" He laughs.

"Seriously. How have I never eaten here?" I smile wide.

Everett appears so carefree as he props himself up on his elbow atop the blanket. We sit beneath a grand oak tree. Its massive branches shade us from the summer sun. A gentle breeze dances around us, only adding to the day's perfection.

"It's a pretty park," I say.

"Yeah, I love it here. It's better this time of year when most of the students aren't in classes. Once the semester starts up, it can get crowded. But it's in the most perfect place…walking distance from all the good eateries and our apartment."

He looks at Benny, who's kicking her legs and flapping her arms as she looks up above, and he smiles.

"She likes the light variations," I tell him. "The contrast between the sky and branches. She gets just as excited over ceiling fans or light fixtures with dark outlines."

"That's cute," he answers.

"That she is."

"What do you think of this one?" He drops a spoonful from a new dish onto my plate.

I take a bite. "It's good," I say. "Not as good as the other dishes but still very tasty."

He shakes his head. "Yeah, that's the only one I'm not a fan of. Stuffed grape leaves. Not my thing."

"They have a distinct flavor for sure."

A guy walks past us, stopping at another large tree a few feet away, and takes a seat against the wide oak.

"Must be taking summer courses," Everett says.

The guy has all the looks of a UofM student with his backpack, metal water bottle, and white AirPods in his ears. The giant textbook he pulls from his backpack only confirms it.

Everett looks at the guy a moment longer. "I must admit, on nice fall days, I do enjoy bringing my laptop and getting some work done here, even with all the students. Something about seeing them all study so intently leaves me relieved. I loved college, but I'm so glad that part of it is over. You know? The stress of tests and assignments—I don't miss that one bit."

"I never went to college," I state. "I started modeling when I was fifteen, and my career took off. I was too busy to go to college, but I was making good money, so I didn't mind. I do think about what that college experience would've been like, though. All of my American friends had it and loved that part of their lives."

"It was definitely fun, no doubt. But to be honest, a

lot of the classes were a waste of time. You have to take so many courses to get a degree that don't really apply to your interests or future career. The social life is what made college great for me."

"Yeah, I heard that part's fun. You and Asher were in a fraternity, right? Quinn has told me a little about them."

He sits up. "Yeah, we were roommates in the frat house. That's how we met and have been best friends since."

"Is it like the movies with like hazing and stuff?"

He grins. "There was hazing, but nothing dangerous or illegal. It was good fun."

"What was it for? Like the purpose of it?" I ask.

"It's for new pledges before they officially become fraternity members. I think, more than anything, it's tradition. It usually took place in what we call hell week, which was the week before initiation."

I lean in. "What types of things did you do?"

"It's top secret." He winks. "If I tell you, I'd have to kill you."

"Seriously?"

"No." He laughs. "Well, not the killing part. It is supposed to be kept secret, but I'll tell ya, anyway."

I clap my hands together. "Great."

"So let's see…they made us put on tutus, and then dropped us off a couple of miles away from campus, and we had to walk back to the house like that. We drank several beers, and then each had to complete a jigsaw puzzle."

I chuckle. "Those are both ridiculous."

"Yeah," he agrees. "There were also chore types of things. Like we had to clean all the toilets in the frat house for a month, and take out the garbage, and do another brother's laundry or carry his backpack."

"Well, those don't sound fun," I admit.

"The chores weren't as fun as the drunken puzzles, that's for sure. We had some responsible hazing, like we were all assigned a weekend when we couldn't drink at all in case any of our frat brothers needed a ride when they were drunk."

"Oh, very responsible," I tease.

"Very." He grins.

"Well, that's good. I'm glad they didn't tie you up and put you on a railroad track as a train was coming and have you untie yourself and escape before your untimely death." I chuckle.

"God, no. I wouldn't have done it if it was like that. I don't want to be part of any organization that puts my life in danger. Nothing is worth that."

I pick up Benny and set her in my lap. "I hope Benny gets your brains. You must be super smart. I heard it's really hard to get into U of M. You have to have top scores in everything to get accepted."

"That's true, about the scores. But just because you didn't go to college doesn't mean you're not brilliant."

"I have my moments." I shrug, suppressing a grin.

"You're brilliant. I can tell, and I hope Benny's just like you."

His words cause my chest to fill with so much adoration for this man. He makes me feel good. I love it and, at the same time, hate it. The last time a man made me feel like this, I was suckered into a marriage from hell. How can I trust my gut when it's let me down before?

My stare drops to his mouth and his full kissable lips. I want his lips on mine more than I want anything else right now, but I promised myself I'd refrain. He's a sexy man hunk that lulls me into a false sense of security every time he touches me. One kiss, and I'd promise him everything I have.

Stick to the plan.

No kisses. No touching.

I blow out a sigh and startle when Everett starts to laugh loudly.

I hold my hand to my chest. "Oh, my gosh. What's so funny?"

"You."

I narrow my gaze. "Why?"

"You know…you made the rules. You can break 'em."

"I don't want to break them," I retort.

He raises his brows. "Could've fooled me."

"What?" My question comes out in a high-pitched voice.

"Just admit you want me to kiss you." He smirks.

"No." My response is less than believable. But I don't need Everett to believe it because we both know that, of course, I want him to kiss me. I simply need to give this torrent of lust a moment to abate.

I hold Benny closer, reminding myself why I need to keep a clear head around Everett.

He leans forward, his face inching closer to my own. I freeze, unable to move. When his lips are a mere heartbeat from my own, he dips his chin and kisses the top of Benny's head.

"Don't worry. Your rules are safe with me." He sits back on the blanket. "I won't touch you again until you ask me to."

I clear my throat. "I'm not going to…ask you."

"Okay," he says, seemingly unaffected.

I hear the truth in his voice just as I feel it in my heart.

I'm a liar, and we both know it.

CHAPTER 17

EVERETT

Cat, Benny, and I spent the day walking around the aquarium in Detroit. It seemed like an appropriate family-friendly outing, but Benny wasn't really into it. She was more obsessed with her own foot than she was any of the fish. I suppose she's just a little too young yet.

I hope I'm with her when she starts becoming more aware of the world around her. I imagine watching a baby discover and learn about her surroundings would be incredible to witness.

Every day, I'm weighed down by the possibility that I won't be there to experience all her firsts, and it's heavy. I'm doing everything I can to show Cat that we're meant to be together, but I don't know if it's working. She's hard to read and has been keeping to her no kissing rule, which, quite honestly, blows. I want to kiss her every second I'm with her, and I hate that I can't.

Tonight, we're staying in and hanging out across the hall at Cassie's place. It's our standing friend date. We get together every week for dinner and to watch *Survivor*. It's not going to be a magnificent date like some of the ones we've had and are going to have. But it's important for Cat to see all sides of me. I want her to pick me and choose us, but I want it to last, too. Life isn't one spectacular date after the next. Sometimes, it's hanging out and watching quality reality TV, and she needs to love that side, too.

Plus, I'd be lying if I said that I didn't tell Cassie and Asher to talk me up, big time. They better not disappoint.

We stand in the hallway between Cassie's and our apartment. We're the only two apartments in the space above the coffee shop, and it works out that we're best friends.

"So you do this every week?" Cat asks.

"Yes, we do. Usually, Tannon and her husband and baby are here, too. But her baby isn't feeling well tonight. So they're staying home. Sometimes, Quinn and Ollie come. But, of course, they're still on their honeymoon. So tonight you have Cassie, her boyfriend, Bennett, Asher, and then us three."

"I've never watched *Survivor*," she says.

"It's okay. We love to talk *Survivor*, so we'll gladly fill you in." I reach for the handle. "You ready?"

Cat nods, and I open the door.

We're greeted by a round of hellos. Cassie walks toward Cat and gives her a hug. "I'm so glad you could make it, and Everett is sooo great. He's absolutely incredible. Isn't he?"

"Smooth, Cass," I grumble with a roll of my eyes.

"What? You told us to talk you up. I'm talking you up," she quips, causing Cat to laugh.

I shake my head. "What's for dinner?" I ask, setting Benny's carrier down by the couch. I unbuckle her seat belt and pick her up.

"Oh, my gosh. That's the best part," Cassie exclaims. "It was Tannon and Jude's turn to cook but you know Eli is sick so they couldn't come. But Jude still dropped off dinner." She turns her attention to Cat. "Jude is the best cook, especially when it comes to Mexican food. He made his abuela's enchilada recipe, and let me tell you, they are heaven. He made a cheese version and a sautéed veggie version for you."

"That sounds great," Cat says.

Asher and Cassie's boyfriend, Bennett, are already at the table shoveling chips and salsa into their mouths.

"Everything's ready. We should dish up." Cassie grins.

We fill our plates and take a seat at the table. Cat

urges me to put Benny in her carrier while we eat, but I don't mind holding her. In fact, I love it. Plus, I can eat with one hand, no problem.

"So Everett has told me some, but I'd love to hear how everyone knows each other," Cat says.

"Well, E, Ash, Tannon, and I met at college. You know? Our sorority and their fraternity were close and held lots of events together. The four of us just kind of gravitated toward one another and became close. We've always had this really great chemistry as friends. It was effortless, really. So when we moved off-campus and found these apartments, it was meant to be. I've loved living across the hall from my besties. Tannon lived here, too, of course, before Jude."

"And Bennett?" Cat asks.

Cassie shakes her head and releases a chuckle. "Oh, yeah. Bennett and I actually met through Jude. They work together."

Bennett nods in agreement and gives Cassie a sweet smile.

I've personally always found the guy a little boring but then again, so was her boyfriend before him. Prior to Bennett, she was dating the manager at Starbucks, Henry, and I'd rather watch paint dry than hang out with that dude. So Bennett's an improvement, at least.

Cassie asks Cat some questions while the other two guys and I shove food into our mouths. Cassie wasn't lying. Jude is one of the best cooks around.

Dinner is carefree and fun. Of course, Cassie could talk to anyone. She's a very easy person to get along with.

"Can I hold the baby?" she asks me, extending her arms.

"Sure." I hand over Benny.

"Hey, cutie-patootie." She kisses Benny's cheeks. "Oh, by the way," she says to everyone else, "boys do the dishes."

"What?" Asher grumbles.

"It's always been the rule. Whoever didn't cook has to clean up," she says.

"Well, that would be everyone here then," Asher says.

Cassie shakes her head. "No, I can't. I'm holding the baby. And Cat's a guest. So go…" She swishes her hand toward the kitchen.

I stand from the table and start clearing people's dishes. "Come on, guys."

"You just asked to hold the baby." Asher narrows his eyes toward Cassie.

She smiles coyly. "I don't know what you're implying, but *Survivor* is waiting, so please get to your job."

"You know you're not going to win against her," I remind him.

"I know." He sighs. "But that doesn't mean I don't like to complain about it."

Bennett volunteers to load the dishwasher and wash

the pans while Asher packages everything up and cleans off the table and counters.

"Everything seems to be going well?" Asher whispers as I scoop the leftover enchiladas into a glass storage container.

"Yeah, I think so." I shrug.

"So you think you two will be a couple or what?"

"I don't know," I say with a shake of my head. "I sure hope so. That's the desired outcome, at least."

"Well, there's real chemistry between you both," he says.

"Right?"

"Definitely." He grins before looking back and forth between Bennett and me. "Well, it looks like you two have it covered, so I'm going to set up the TV."

"You're ridiculous." I laugh.

A few moments later, we're sitting on the sofa sectional watching *Survivor* and passing around Benny. She's such a chill baby. I love it.

"Oh, no!" Cassie says when one of the contestants shows her "ally" her hidden immunity necklace.

"Why is that a bad thing?" Cat asks. "Aren't they friends?"

"The dude is only pretending to be her ally. Now that he knows she has an immunity necklace, he's going to target her to get her out before she can use it. But he'll continue to pretend that he's in her alliance until he rallies votes to get her out. That way, she won't see it coming," I say.

"It will be an epic blindside," Asher states.

"That sounds mean," Cat says.

"It is." Cassie chuckles. "People can get cutthroat when playing for a million dollars."

"Money isn't worth tarnishing your character and hurting your friends," Cat says.

"To many—especially those who don't have it—it is," Asher states. "Plus, they just met these people a week ago. They're not close friends."

"I don't like it. It's not nice," Cat says.

"It's *Survivor*, baby." I wrap my arm around her shoulder and pull her against my side. She leans in, and it feels so right. I can picture the two of us just hanging out, watching our shows, in the future.

Cat's attention is glued to the screen during tribal council, and she gasps when the obvious blindside happens.

"Told ya," Asher says. "Never reveal you have an idol."

After the show has ended, we say our goodbyes. Asher follows us out to the hall, leaving Cassie and Bennett in the apartment.

"Thanks for hanging out tonight, Cat. See you around," Asher says to Cat before heading into our apartment and leaving us in the hallway.

"So..." I stand before Cat and rub her arms. "What'd you think?"

"It was fun," she says. "Your friends are so nice and hilarious. It was a great time. I can see the appeal of your show, but still…it's mean."

"Never said it wasn't." I chuckle. "But you'll get used to it."

Her gaze holds mine, and we share a weighted stare.

"Do you want to come in?" I ask. "You can stay here. You can have my room if you want. I'll sleep on the couch."

She shakes her head. "No, it's okay. Really. All the baby's stuff is set up over at Alma's. It's just easier."

"Okay, well…thanks for hanging out tonight. I loved having you there. It felt like you were always meant to be there. You know?"

"Things are pretty effortless with us, and I can't decide if it's real." She bites her lip.

"It's real." My gaze drops to her lips before returning to her eyes. "It's real. You just have to trust it. Take the leap of faith."

She raises her arm and cups my cheek. "I used to be the type of girl who would take the leap, but that's no longer me."

"It could be."

"No." She sighs, dropping her hand. "I can't live off feelings anymore. I need the facts. I must be sure, without a doubt. I don't want to fail again. I know I sound like a broken record, and I'm sorry. But I'm not ready to make any decisions."

I tilt my face down and kiss her forehead. "It's okay. We still have time. You don't have to make any decisions yet."

She nods.

"Just remember that sometimes in love and life, you'll never get irrefutable answers. Sometimes, you have to trust that everything will work out."

"I'm trying, Ev. I am. In my heart, I know that you're good for me, for us." She looks toward our sleeping daughter. "But the walls I've built refuse to fall."

I take her face between my hands and lean in until I can feel her breath against my lips. "Just give the word. I could bring down those walls. Easy."

She lifts a finger and presses it against my lips, taking a step back. "I know you could."

I drop my hands to my sides. "I'll see you tomorrow?"

"Tomorrow," she agrees.

Every step she takes away from me intensifies the unsettled feeling that resides deep within my gut. She gives me a final wave at the bottom of the stairs and exits the building.

Bringing my hands to my head, I comb them through my hair with a sigh.

It's okay. I still have time.

I remind myself to have faith, but that's hard to do when my future depends on someone's choice.

Choose wisely, Cat.

CHAPTER 18

CAT

*E*very muscle in my body is relaxed, and my skin is softer than silk. This morning, Everett dropped me off at a fancy spa while he hung out with Benny.

I've been thoroughly pampered and massaged.

The skin treatments were out of this world. I'm positive my skin has never felt so amazing. I can't recall the name of them all, but there was wax, seaweed, and even some posh mud involved in the series of skin therapies. I've heard about the healing properties of mud but must admit that I was a skeptic. Until now. I'm a full-on convert. Cover me with dirt any day.

If I lived in Ann Arbor, I'd have a weekly standing

appointment for this place. They'd own me. I'm a believer.

Do I feel bad that Everett is going above and beyond to show me he cares? A little bit, yes. I don't need him to shower me with gifts or take me on swoon-worthy adventures to get to know him as a person—which is all I really need. I want to truly know the man who helped in the creation of my daughter. Plain and simple. The rest…is unnecessary.

At the same time, I'd be lying if I said I wasn't enjoying every second. I mean, my skin has never been softer.

The sun warms my face as I exit the spa. It's a beautiful Michigan summer day. I must admit, I miss the weather here. People often complain about the winters, but it's the seasons I love. Each one is perfect and unique, carrying attributes that I love.

Everett waits in his parked car in the circle pickup loop in front of the building.

I open the passenger door and glance toward the back, where Benny sleeps in her car seat. "Have you been waiting long?" I ask, closing the door behind me.

"Nope. Not long at all. How was it?" He gifts me with a smile, and my heartbeat quickens.

I buckle the seat belt and clear my throat. "Good. No, great. I loved everything about it."

"I knew you would." There's pure happiness in his voice.

"So what's the plan? Have a low-key rest of the day?" I question.

He scoffs. "It's like you don't know me at all. You brought the items I suggested, right?"

"Yep. They're in my bag in the back."

"Good."

"Are you going to tell me why I need to bring baby blankets and jeans in the middle of summer?" I grin.

"You'll see."

"You're obsessed with surprises." I chuckle. "They give you life."

"No truer words have ever been spoken." He shoots me a wink.

"Alright, I trust you," I say.

"That's all I ask," he says with a smile as he pulls out of the parking lot.

* * *

"No one else is here," I note as I scan the ice rink, thankful that I had pants and a jacket to change into.

"Nope. I'm friends with the owner, Bill. I designed and maintain his website. He's a really cool dude. I asked if he'd open it up for me, and he agreed."

"So we have the whole place to ourselves for the entire afternoon?"

"That we do," he says. "Have you been ice skating before?"

I nod. "Yeah, but not since I was a kid."

"They have those walker things you can push around if you need help." He raises a brow.

I shake my head. "Are you kidding me? I don't think so."

"What?" He chuckles. "There's no shame in getting a little help if you need it."

"I'll be fine."

I finish lacing up my skates and look over at Benny. She's fed and changed and happily napping in her carrier, cozy beneath a blanket. She really is such a *good baby*, as they like to say.

Everett waves toward a window at the top of the rink, and the first few notes of a guitar solo sound out. I release a yelp of surprise and bring my hand to my chest, causing Everett to laugh.

"I made a playlist for our skating adventure," he says.

"A playlist?"

"Yep," he says, stepping onto the ice. He skates backward with ease as he extends his hand toward mine. He's definitely been on the ice before. "I composed some of my favorite rock ballads for our romantic skate date." He puckers his lips, and I can't help but grin at his cuteness.

Hesitantly, arms out to my side for balance, I step onto the ice. "What's this song?"

His eyes go wide. "You don't know this song?"

I shake my head.

"Ugh," he groans. "It's one of the best. Mr. Big, 'Wild World.'" He says the title with emphasis as if hearing it will trigger a long-lost memory of this song, but it doesn't. "From 1993."

"That's the year I was born." I laugh.

"I know, but surely your parents played it. My mom had the CD. She loved it."

"Remember, I didn't come to the States until I was eighteen, and my parents weren't big into American rock ballads." I smile.

He nods. "Gotcha…well, then, we have some work to do." He continues to skate backward. With his arms raised, he sings, "Ooo, baby, baby. It's a wild world…"

Skating circles around me, he belts out the lyrics to the song, and my face hurts from smiling so wide. I've never heard this song, but it just may be my new favorite song ever. Maybe it's the lyrics, or Everett's crazy rendition, or the fact that a beautiful boy is serenading me on ice skates, but my heart turns to utter mush.

An instrumental with a guitar and some "la-la's" play, and Everett raises his hands in the air and sways them to the music. "It's good, right?" He grins as he stops his backward descent and starts toward me. His grasp holds my waist, and he whips behind me. "You're doing great. But how about we go a little faster?"

I release a scream and grab onto his forearms as he propels us forward. My legs freeze and allow Everett to guide us around the rink. The cool air hits my face as Everett's strong body moves behind me, pushing us around the rink.

Releasing my death grip on his arms, I lean back, pushing my own arms out to the side. Closing my eyes, I let go of all my control, giving it to Everett.

"There you go." His husky whisper against my ear causes goose bumps to pebble on my skin.

It's my own *Titanic* moment on ice, and it fills my soul.

Another song starts, and Everett takes my hand in his and guides us around the rink, our legs pushing off with each beat. I feel like a kid, so carefree. I'm a novice on skates, but my hand in his gives me the courage to be fearless—something I haven't been in a very long time.

We skate hand in hand, vibing to the music. Some of the music I've heard before, while some of it is new to me. Somehow, it's all perfect. It's as if Everett always knows what I need.

After a dozen songs, I ask, "So old rock ballads are your thing?"

"Music is my thing. I love it all. Rap, oldies, rock, pop, and sometimes even country. It just depends on my mood. I've never been the person who favors one genre of music because each type lends itself to different emotions. Like right now. What do you feel?"

I think about it. "Happy. Carefree. Hopeful...and a little...gushy and lovey inside."

"Yes." He laughs. "Exactly what I was going for. See?"

I nod. "Yeah, I see."

"Cassie and Tannon always make fun of Asher and me because the music at our parties is completely different from week to week. But it's not by chance. They think it's a random selection, but it's completely thought out. It's always dependent on the vibe I'm aiming for."

"I can see that. Music does have that effect. I just think maybe your tastes are more eclectic than others," I offer.

"Oh, definitely. Music is like a religion to me. I study and analyze it. I love it."

"Why didn't you go into something in the music field?" I wonder.

He laughs. "You heard me sing a bit ago, right? Just because I love it doesn't mean I'm skilled at it. I can't sing or play any instrument. Believe me, I've tried them all." He shrugs. "The productive part of my brain thrives on the analytical stuff, computers, software, and code. It comes easily. The artsy side of my brain, the part that adores music, isn't dominant. But it's the part I love the most, and that's why I work so hard at it, dissecting songs and rhythms, and deciphering how they make me feel. It's fun."

"See, that's me and clothes. Every item I wear makes me feel a certain way."

"I get that." He nods. "So maybe your artistic side is

visual, and you find joy in the way things, like clothes, look. And I feel emotions through sounds. Not that I've studied that aspect or anything, but I bet there's something to it."

"I bet there is," I agree. "So any future parties we hold…I'll be in charge of the décor and you, the music?"

"Future parties?" he questions, happiness in his voice.

"Maybe." I shrug. "I guess we'll see. So you never did explain how you're so skilled on the ice?"

He releases my hand and darts forward, swinging his arms back and forth like he's holding an imaginary stick. He stops quickly, pushing the blades of his skates to the side with a spray of ice. "That would be from hockey. Played ice hockey from the time I was five until I graduated from high school."

"I didn't know that," I say.

"Yeah." He shrugs. "I went to a birthday party for one of my classmates in kindergarten that was held at an arena. His name was Sawyer, and his parents were really into ice hockey. Sawyer's dad, Jimmy, played in college, and I guess was good enough to go pro. Long story short, he didn't because Sawyer's mom got pregnant, and he decided to get a steady job and raise a family. Anyway, it was my first time on skates, and I was a natural, so Jimmy told my mom that she should get me into the sport. When she explained that she couldn't afford it, Jimmy took me under his wing and sponsored me for the next thirteen years."

"Oh, wow."

"Yeah." Everett nods. "An injury to my knee during my senior year killed that dream."

"What about Sawyer? Did he follow in his dad's footsteps?"

He shakes his head. "No. Ended up hating the sport."

"Aw, that's too bad. Do you see Jimmy much anymore?"

Everett blows out a sigh. "No, he passed away from cancer shortly after my injury."

"I'm sorry," I say.

"Yeah, he was an amazing guy."

I blow out a breath. "You are an amazing guy. What can't you do?"

"What do you mean?" He grins.

"You're a computer whiz, a music buff, a love expert, and an ice hockey star."

"I don't know about all that." He chuckles before quirking a brow. "Expand on the love expert part."

My cheeks blush. "I'm just saying, you always seem to know exactly what to say and do to make an outing really special…to make me feel really special."

"So it's working?" He lifts his brows.

"The verdict is still out, but I'll say that the jurors are very happy."

He skates up beside me and extends his hand. I entwine my fingers through his once more. "Well, for now, that's enough," he says.

CHAPTER 19

EVERETT

The warm summer night comes with just enough cool wind for a light blanket. I love the feeling of Cat beside me, her leg pressed against mine beneath the thin covering. Being with her makes me feel incredibly exhilarated as if I've discovered this magical being and am lucky enough to be in her presence. At the same time, it carries a weight or normalcy as if there's nowhere else I was meant to be.

Every moment with Cat is a duel of conflicting emotions. Gratitude and relief. Calmness and nervousness. But the one constant is love. I freaking love every second we're together.

"Cheers." Cat holds a glass of wine up and taps it against my bottle of beer.

"Cheers."

She chuckles under her breath and takes a sip of wine. "This is amazing, Ev. Like, truly one of the best dates I've ever had."

Her words fill my chest with hope. "I'm glad."

"You know I've never been to a drive-in movie theater." She leans back in the plush loveseat that I've set up in the back of my friend's truck bed.

I wanted to take Cat on an ordinary all-American date. What's more normal than dinner and a movie? Yet I had our daughter to consider. So I opted for takeout and a drive-in movie. Benny spent the first half of the date on a cushy blanket we laid out in the truck bed while we ate sushi. After dinner, Cat nursed her, and Benny fell right asleep. She's now dreaming comfortably in her baby carrier in the cab of the truck while Cat and I are enjoying the movie on the giant screen before us—sort of.

I'm enjoying the date. Absolutely. But the movie? I've barely watched it. Most of our time has been spent talking. It's funny…one of my biggest pet peeves is people who talk throughout a movie. Yet Cat and I haven't stopped talking, and I'm not bothered in the least.

"I know. You lived here for a long time. I can't believe you didn't go at least once," I respond. "I mean, it's a classic American experience."

"Is it still, though?" Cat asks. "I mean, drive-ins aren't very popular anymore. They're shutting down everywhere."

"Yeah, that's true...and sad. I grew up going to drive-in movies. There was this theater near our apartment that didn't charge for children. So it was a perfect activity for those living on a budget. My mom only had to pay for herself, and she would pack so many snacks. In all my time growing up, I never had food from the concessions. I know now that it's because it was too expensive. At the time, I just thought my mom brought better snacks. Plus, they always had back-to-back movies. So it was a good four-to-five-hour activity."

"Those sound like amazing memories." Cat plops a cheese cracker into her mouth.

I nod. "They are."

"Is it bad that I don't feel guilty about eating these?" She scrunches her nose.

"Not at all." I laugh. "I can't believe you've never eaten a Cheez-it, Cat. I mean...have you even lived without having tried the 'crack crackers.'"

"Normally, I'd disagree with you...but you're right. They are like crack. I could eat the whole box and never get full." She plops another cracker in her mouth and shrugs her shoulder. "I know they're probably horrible for me, but I can't find it in me to care at the moment. They're so delicious...and with wine!"

I throw my head back and laugh. "I know...Cassie

and Tannon, my besties from across the hall, used to swear that Cheez-its and wine were the best combination."

"I mean, I'll never buy them. They're not part of my diet, and I know I couldn't handle the temptation. But I sure am enjoying them now."

"Well, I'm glad I could provide a couple of first-time experiences for you tonight."

"Me too." She scoots closer and leans her head against my shoulder.

I circle my arm around her shoulders and pull her closer. Her warmth against me feels so right. She's everything I want in a partner. I'd give anything to lean in and kiss her, but she asked me not to, so I won't. I'm keeping my promise. I won't kiss her until she asks me to. I just wish she'd ask me already because I'm dying to taste her again.

"I love romantic comedies," she says, looking forward at the large screen.

Honestly, I'd been so wrapped up in her that I couldn't tell you what the movie playing was about. I know now. It's a romance of some sort. Truthfully, they're not my thing—a little too cheesy for me—but I could watch the hell out of a predictable love story every night of the week if I had Cat at my side.

She continues, "I actually learned a lot of my English watching old-school love stories from the eighties."

"Oh, yeah?"

She nods. "Yep, *Sixteen Candles* was one of my favorites. Then there's *Overboard* with Goldie Hawn and Kurt Russell that I watched more than I'd care to admit."

"Like are we talking five times? Ten?"

"At minimum, like fifty." She chuckles.

"You've watched *Overboard* fifty times?"

"At least. One of my favorite lines was, 'Everyone wants to be me!'" she says in a high-pitched voice.

I laugh. "I think I've seen it like once…I don't remember that line."

"Oh, it's seriously the best. I used to skip around the house chanting it. I bet I annoyed the crap out of my parents. I'm pretty sure Goldie's character's rich outfits started my love affair with clothes."

"We'll have to watch it sometime," I suggest.

"Definitely." She takes a sip of her wine. "I will say my favorite moment was from *Say Anything* when John Cusack held up that boom box and played, 'In Your Eyes'…Ugh…melted my heart every time. I wanted to marry him."

"John Cusack?"

"Yeah."

"He's like twenty years older than you." I laugh.

"Twenty-six and it didn't matter because it was true love." She grins.

"You fell in love with great storytelling." I shake my head. "Probably not actually John himself."

She shrugs. "Maybe you're right. But seriously? Is there anything more romantic than that scene?"

I bite my lip, shaking my head. "I don't think I've seen it."

With a gasp, Cat playfully hits me on the arm. "Seriously, Everett. You're missing out."

I laugh. "Sorry. I think that movie was a little before my time."

"But it's a classic."

"I'll watch it at some point. Okay?"

"Okay." She nudges my leg with her knee. "You better."

A sappy love song plays, and the credits roll across the screen. "Oh, that was so good."

"We barely watched it." I chuckle.

"Hey, I watched it. I can multitask."

"Well, apparently, I can't...or maybe I'm just too enthralled with my beautiful date to pay attention."

She ignores my comment. "So there's really another one right after?"

"Yeah, I think the next one is about a shark attack, a thriller of some sort."

Setting her empty wineglass down, she pulls her knees up onto the sofa and holds them against her chest. "Really? That seems like a horrible pairing. To go from romance to shark attacks?"

"I know." I grin. "But I guess they figure people can

leave if they don't want to watch the second movie. Do you want to leave?"

She shakes her head. "No way. I'm having too much fun."

"Good. Me too."

We compare the qualities of a Red Vine versus a Twizzler while we wait for the next movie to start. For some reason, I knew that Cat wouldn't have tried either, and I needed her to decide which one she liked better.

"So this is important?" she questions.

"Yes. You're either a Red Vine person or a Twizzler person. I need to know where you stand," I tease.

"And they're both licorice? They taste very different."

I pull another Red Vine out of the plastic packaging and hand it to her. "Technically, neither are really licorice. Only black licorice has any licorice root in it, but they're referred to as licorice…yes."

She chews carefully. "They're both edible." She shrugs.

"Yes. But which one do you enjoy more?"

"Which is your favorite?" she asks.

"No way. You need to reach your own conclusion without my bias," I say.

She laughs again. "So this is serious business?"

"Absolutely." I nod.

"Okay." She takes another bite of the Twizzler and chews it completely before swallowing and doing the same with the Red Vine. "I've made my decision," she declares. "I don't know why…so don't ask me to explain. But I like the Red Vine better."

"Yes!" I cheer a little too loudly. I squeeze her into a side hug. Lowering my voice, I say, "I knew we were compatible. Everyone is a Twizzler fan, and I don't get it because Red Vines are so much better."

She giggles and takes another bite of the Red Vine. "I'm glad you approve of my decision."

"I mean, I'd love you regardless, but it does make me proud that you made the right choice." There's a moment of awkward air between us at my mention of the l-word. I defuse the tension by holding out a Red Vine and hitting it against hers in a weird licorice sword fight. "Cheers."

"Cheers." She smiles and takes another bite.

"I think it's the texture for me. It's more closely related to gummy bears than licorice," I offer.

"Maybe that's it."

The low notes indicating that something dreadful is about to happen start to play from the portable speaker I have sitting at our feet. The movie opens with a shot of the deep ocean. It's eerie and suspenseful. Out of nowhere, there's a frame of a giant shark on the screen, and Cat yelps, burying her face against my arm.

"You going to make it?" I huff out a laugh.

"I'm not a fan of scary movies," she admits.

"We can leave?" I offer again.

"No, I want to stay. Just protect me from any sharks

that jump from the screen." She peeks out and releases a sigh when she sees the movie has moved on to the characters drinking piña coladas on an island beach.

"I can do that," I promise. "You know, we could pass the time with some other activities?" I suggest, my tone coy.

"Like?"

"Well, besides eating, drinking, and talking at the drive-in. There's usually a lot of making out."

She pushes my arm. "Everett," she whines. "I told you that's off-limits."

I raise my hands in surrender. "Fine. I'm just saying...it could be another first tonight."

She turns to me, her big green eyes capturing mine. "You know it's not that I don't want to. Right? Because I do. I *really* do. But we can't. If I'm going to figure this out and make the right decision, I need a clear head. You understand that, right?"

The pressure in my chest builds, and emotion rises. I press my thumb against her plump bottom lip. "I do." I sigh.

She kisses the pad of my thumb and holds my hand in hers. "If I forget to tell you later, I want you to know how amazing tonight has been."

"Good." The corner of my lips tilts in a smile.

"You make every moment so special," she says before releasing my hand and facing forward to return her attention to the screen once more.

"So is it all scary movies or just ones with sharks?" I ask, circling my arm around her shoulders.

"All of them. Not a fan."

"Noted." I softly squeeze her shoulders, and she leans back into my side.

The closer I get with Cat, the further away I feel. I don't know what else to do.

All I can do is be myself, but I have this sinking feeling it won't be enough. The unspoken countdown in the background serves as a continuous reminder that our time together is coming to an end.

I'm running out of time, and she's still not mine.

CHAPTER 20

CAT

I squeeze into my skinny jeans and suck in as I button them. Everyone says that I look the same—as if I didn't just have a baby a few months ago. Although their words are sweet, they are very much mistaken. My body has definitely changed. I probably couldn't get runway work now, even if I wanted to.

It's honestly fine, though. I grew a life within me for a good part of a year. That's an incredible accomplishment, and I'm so proud of my body for being strong and creating something as magnificent as my baby Bernadette. It's only natural that it should change. I just need to buy new jeans is all.

Everett said tonight was a "jeans date," so here I am

in jeans. He didn't specify footwear, so I'm opting for my black Manolo Blahnik pointed-toe pumps because they look hot with jeans. Anyone who knows me knows that footwear is my favorite part of the outfit.

As I peer into the full-length mirror, the reflection staring back is one of pure happiness. This trip, this place, these people…are all so good for me. I can't help but be happy. I've loved being back in my father's home country with my family over the past year, but I can't deny how very much I've missed Michigan. Despite the heartache it brought me, it gave me so much more. A home. Family.

I opt for a small Tiffany's chain necklace with an open-heart pendant to complement the simple black tank top I'm wearing. And I'm ready.

Amos and Alma are snuggled up together on the sofa watching what appears to be a reality show.

"What's that?" I snatch my purse from the table and remove my lip gloss from inside.

"Oh my gosh, it's so good." Alma twists back to face me. "These people fall in love just by talking to each other in these pods. They get engaged, sight unseen." She nods, her eyes wide.

"And that works?" I chuckle, applying my lip gloss.

"Sometimes. Yeah. It's crazy."

"It sounds entertaining," I admit.

"Oh, it is. Right, Cookie?" She nudges her husband.

"Very," he deadpans.

I drop the lip gloss back in my purse just as I hear Everett pull in. "So I think she's down for the night. She's been good the last couple of days, sleeping until five in the morning or so. But if she wakes…"

Alma waves her hand in the air. "I'll rock her back to sleep. It will be fine. Go. Have fun."

"But if she doesn't go back to sleep, call me. We're going to be downtown. Just minutes away. I can come back at a moment's notice."

"Oh, my gosh. It will be fine. Seriously, go have fun with your baby daddy. We're good…I promise," Alma says, turning back toward the television.

"Okay…but call me if you need—"

"Bye!" Alma cuts me off.

I open the door to find Everett with his fist raised, about to knock. "Hey." I grin.

"Hey, you." His gaze burns down my entire body. "You look amazing!" He hands me a bouquet in varying shades of pale pink. They're gorgeous.

"Thank you." I take the flowers and bring them to my face, inhaling. "These are beautiful." I turn around and place the flowers on the table in the foyer. "I'm leaving flowers on the table," I call into the house.

I hear Amos. "On it."

I shut the door behind me. "He'll put them in a vase for me." I take in Everett, and my skin heats. He's wearing perfectly fitting jeans and a flannel button-down. It's simple and irresistible at the same time. "You look good," I admit.

He extends his bent elbow, and I loop my arm through. "Yeah, I'd say we're a pretty hot-looking couple."

"Would you?" I chuckle.

"Oh, definitely."

"So where are we going on this mystery date?" I inquire as Everett leads us to the car.

He opens the door for me like a gentleman, and I slide into the seat.

"You'll see, but I think it's something that you haven't done before." The corner of his mouth tilts into a grin as he shuts the door and jogs around the front of the car.

"How is it that I've lived here for so long yet haven't gone to all these places or tried these restaurants?" I ask once he's in the car.

He starts to back out of the drive. "I really don't know what you did when you lived here." He shrugs. "But it's my honor to help you experience it all."

"So noble," I tease.

"That I am." He shoots me a wink, and I must admit it has my insides doing flips.

It's only been a couple of hours since I've seen Everett. He spent the entire day hanging out with Benny and me. Yet I missed him in the two hours we were apart. Real feelings are forming for this man, and I only have a few days to figure out what they mean. The countdown to my departure is constantly in the recesses of my mind, putting pressure on me to decide. But I can't rush this. I have to know for sure.

"You okay?" Everett asks as he pulls into a parking space beside a brick building.

"Yep." I give him a reassuring grin. "Just thinking."

"Okay. Well, we're here," he says before exiting the vehicle and walking around the car to open my door.

I'm a modern woman who doesn't need a man for anything. I've been successful on my own merit since I was just a teen. Yet something about Everett's chivalry melts my heart. It reminds me of the way my father loves my mother.

Everett leads us inside, and I gasp when I see a wall of large targets and people hurling axes over their heads toward the bull's-eye.

"Oh, my gosh...what is this?" I laugh.

"Axe throwing. It's a thing now. Seriously. It's really popular all of a sudden...and it's fun. Come on."

Everett gets us drinks from the bar and leads us to our own little axe throwing area. He sets the beverages on a tall round table. "Have you thrown axes before?"

I shake my head. "No."

He grins proudly, raising a brow. "I knew it'd be a first." He points toward the target. "The object is to get it as close to the red circle in the middle. Each ring out from the red mark is fewer points."

"I haven't thrown axes, but I have lived in this century. I know what the purpose of a target is." I giggle.

He shrugs. "I was just making sure."

Everett demonstrates the proper technique for holding and throwing an axe. I watch as he chucks the medal blade toward the target hitting the red circle.

"So you've obviously done this before," I observe.

"A few times." He retrieves the axe from the wooden target and brings it back for me.

I lift the axe over my head, imitating Everett's form. I feel awkward and off-balance as I hurl the axe forward. The second it's left my grasp, I begin to fall face-first.

I yelp as Everett grabs me by the waist, halting my inevitable tumble toward the floor. "Oh, my gosh, that's hard." I hold Everett to steady myself.

"Well, it probably doesn't help that you're balancing on a two-centimeter-wide spike." He drops his eyes to my pumps.

"They go with my outfit, and you didn't specify footwear," I grumble.

He jogs over to the end of our area, where the axe lays on the floor. I didn't see if I missed the target altogether or didn't have enough force to my throw for it to stick into the wood—I was too busy falling—but regardless, the axe is on the ground. I'm new to this, but I'm guessing that is zero points.

He hands me the axe. "Let's try this again."

This time, he stands behind me, gripping my waist and holding me steady.

I repeat the motion from earlier without the near face-plant, and the blade sticks into the fourth ring from the red center.

Jumping up, I clap my hands together. "I hit it!"

"You did." Everett laughs. "Good job."

We take turns tossing the axe toward the wall, and it's a blast. On what must be my twentieth toss, I hit the bull's-eye. I raise my hands in celebration and turn toward Everett. His hands rest on my hips to keep me steady.

"Who knew I had lumberjack in my DNA?" I drop my arms onto his shoulders and wrap my hands around his neck.

He tightens his hold on my hips, pulling me toward him. "Who knew?" He grins.

I lick my lips as my stare drops to his mouth. His chest rises as he pulls in a breath. My eyes close, and for a moment, I don't care about my rules. I just want to be kissed.

I can't. The rules are there for a reason. I need to figure this out.

I quickly lean into his chest and hug him. "This has been so much fun. Thank you."

He clears his throat. "Of course."

We stand in this embrace for a moment, and then he steps back. "Another drink?" he asks.

"Sure."

I take a seat on the stool as Everett retreats to the bar for more drinks. I shamelessly admire his jean-clad ass as he walks away. "Oh, Cat…what are you doing?" I whisper to myself.

Everett returns and hands me a martini. He brings a beer bottle to his lips and takes a sip.

"Do we have to leave this area so someone else can use it?" I ask.

"No, I rented this spot for a few hours. So whether we're throwing or just sitting here talking…it's ours."

"Ah, I see. So what do you want to talk about?" I take a sip of my martini.

He puckers his lips in thought. "Tell me something that grosses you out."

"What?" I chuckle.

"Yeah, something that you find really disgusting."

I think for a moment. "Okay, well…I have a thing about breath. I hate bad breath, right? I really think people don't spend enough time brushing their tongues. Like, that's where the bacteria are…you know? So when people post pictures of themselves sticking out their tongues, and their tongues are white in the photos…I want to barf."

"Really?" Everett laughs.

"Yeah." I chuckle. "I mean, why would someone post a picture of their white, bacteria-filled tongue? You know they have bad breath."

"That's weird." Everett smiles. "I guess I've never thought about that too much."

"Well, next time you're on social media and someone posts a tongue pic, I guarantee you're going to be looking to see what color their tongue is." I stick out my tongue. "What color is it?"

"Like a light pink," he responds.

I nod. "Exactly. Stick yours out."

"No." He shakes his head.

"Do it." I giggle.

"You're going to judge," he says.

"Of course, I am. I have a thing about breath. I can't help it."

He releases a forced sigh. "Well, it's make or break time, I guess." He sticks out his tongue.

"Pink." I grin. "I already knew yours would be pink. You never have bad breath. If you did, we wouldn't be hanging out as much."

"Harsh," he teases.

"I'm just saying. How hard is it to brush one's tongue? The mouth has more germs than any other place on your body. If a person isn't going to at least try to keep it clean, why am I going to kiss him?"

"I see your point."

"So what is something you find gross?" I ask.

"Puke," he answers.

"Well, obviously." I laugh.

"No, like I can't handle it. If someone vomits, I'm

puking right along with them. It's the smell and"—he makes a disgusted face—"all of it. I hate it. That's why I don't date girls that can't hold their liquor. If I go out with a girl, and she pukes, we're done. No second date."

"Has that happened?" I chuckle.

He rolls his eyes and nods. "Oh, yeah…more times than I care to remember. College girls, or at least the ones that have been interested in me, cannot manage their drinking. It's like puke central. It's one of the things I first admired about you."

"What?" I pull in a sharp breath. "I didn't come close to puking."

"Exactly. That first day in the casino, when we were drinking, you asked for water between drinks. And, I was like, 'man, this girl is a keeper.'"

"It doesn't take much to impress you," I say.

"When it comes to that…no," he agrees.

The two of us chat and laugh over nothing and everything for hours. When I'm with Everett, I feel like I'm with my best friend…who I secretly want to make out with. Surely, that's a good sign.

CHAPTER 21

EVERETT

I park the car in Alma's driveway. Several other vehicles are already in the drive, so I'm assuming we're one of the last ones to arrive.

Ollie and Quinn got back from their honeymoon yesterday, so Alma is hosting a barbecue for everyone to hang out and chat with the newlyweds. It's hard to believe that a week and a half ago, *Daisy* showed up at my friend's wedding, holding my baby. The past ten days have flown by. At the same time, so much has happened that it feels like it's been months since Quinn and Ollie tied the knot.

"This feels weird." Asher unbuckles his seat belt and lifts the bowl of potato salad from his lap. He eyes the dish with a suspicious squint. "We're at the age where we bring a bowl of chopped potatoes and mayonnaise to a party? When did this happen?"

I laugh. "I don't know, man. In the last week, I guess."

"It doesn't feel right."

"I think that's what we're supposed to do? Bring a dish to pass or whatever." I shrug, the corner of my mouth tilting up.

He shakes his head. "I still can't believe you boiled potatoes and chopped shit…and made this. This is all happening too fast," he grumbles.

I step out of the car and shut the door. "I went to Costco. Bought a huge container of the stuff. Dumped it in a bowl, and…now, we're here."

"Ahh." Asher nods his head. "That makes more sense. Okay, I feel better. Now, that seems like something guys our age would do. But can you hold it?" He extends the ceramic bowl toward me. "I can't walk into a party with this."

"You're ridiculous." I chuckle, taking the bowl from Asher.

"I'm just saying, there have been a lot of big changes in the past couple of weeks. I need time to adjust," he says.

I roll my eyes. "Yes, so many new things affecting *your* life."

Alma's husband, Amos, opens the door. "Hey, guys. Come in. Everyone's out back."

"I brought this," I say, handing Amos the bowl of potato salad feeling incredibly awkward.

He eyes the dish. "Thanks." He takes it from me with a smile.

Asher and I walk through the house.

"See...not weird at all," I lie.

"Better you than me." He scoffs.

We step onto the back deck. Alma and Quinn are chatting away on the corner of the deck, a glass of wine in their hands. I'm sure they're gushing over details of the honeymoon. Tannon, Jude, and their baby, Eli, are in the yard with Alma's daughter, Love. They're holding giant bubble wands and blowing huge bubbles for Eli to chase—or wobble toward. Cassie and her boyfriend, Bennett, stand back and watch.

Ollie sits on the porch swing with a red-headed girl, who appears to be in her late teens or early twenties, who I haven't met. Alma's mother, Lee-Anne, and who I can only assume is her boyfriend are standing in front of the grill, turning veggie kabobs over the flames.

There's a round of waves and greetings when our presence is noted.

"Oh, my God. We've landed in picturesque suburbia," Asher says.

I shrug. "Well, we are almost thirty. We were bound to grow out of apartment keg parties at some point."

Asher shoots me a glare. "Speak for yourself. Anyway, want a beer?"

"Sure," I say, as Amos comes out of the house with a platter of raw steaks.

"How do you guys want them cooked?" he asks.

"Medium, please."

"You got it." He nods and heads toward the grill.

Cat follows Amos, coming from inside the house, with Benny in her arms.

"There you two are." I smile, my entire soul happier at the sight of my girls.

"Hey." Cat smiles. "I was inside changing her diaper."

I pull my girls into a hug and take Benny into my arms. "How's your day been?"

"Good. I visited with some of my past work friends. They all wanted to see Benny."

I raise a brow. "Past work friends as in…models."

Cat chuckles. "Most of them, yes."

"Well, let's keep that from Asher. The last thing we need is him wanting you to set him up to go out on a double date with us."

"We're safe. They're all taken—either married or in committed relationships." She grins.

"Oh, that's good."

Asher returns and hands me a bottle of beer. "Hey, Cat. Hey, baby," he says, putting his finger out for Benny to grab. "Do you guys want to play some cornhole? I mean, if we're going traditional Midwestern barbecue here, we need to play. Amos told me they had some boards here in the garage."

"I've never played," Cat admits.

"Another first." I extend my hand, and she takes it. I can't hide the smile across my face. I'd give anything to kiss her, but if hand holding is all I get, I'll take it. "It's easy."

We follow Asher to the garage. I release Cat's hand to grab one of the boards. They're nice ones, made of real wood, and therefore, heavy.

"We need a fourth," I say as I follow Asher across the yard with the board in my grasp.

"Cassie. Cornhole. Now!" Asher calls out in an obnoxious tone causing me to laugh.

"Coming!" Cassie leaves the group that's blowing bubbles and meets us where we've set up the board. "Hey, you guys made it."

"Well, Martha Stewart here had to make potato salad first," Asher teases, hiking a thumb in my direction.

"Really? Ambitious." Cassie grins with a satisfied nod.

"Hardly." I shake my head. "I cheated."

She smiles knowingly. "Ah, gotcha. Store-bought."

"Absolutely."

"There's no shame in that," she says.

"So how does this game work?" Cat asks as she takes the long scarf thing she uses and wraps Benny against her chest.

"You're like Superwoman," I tell her, motioning toward the baby she carries with ease.

"It's not hard." She grins, carefree and effortlessly. "She likes being close to me, plus it frees up my hands to play." She waves her hands out to the side.

Asher explains the game to her, which doesn't take long.

"It's pretty simple then. Get the beanbag in the hole of your board," Cat summarizes. "Two points if it lands in the hole, one point if it lands on the board…and we're playing to twenty-one."

"Yep. Pretty straightforward," I say, moving the wooden board on the ground to face the one across from it.

"So teams…me and Cass against you two?" Asher suggests.

"Sounds good." I drop four blue-colored beanbags in Asher's hands, leaving Cat and me with the yellow.

The fabric of the bags has the University of Michigan block M's across the blue and maize bags, representing our alma mater's colors. Ann Arbor has no shortage of pride when it comes to our university.

Once we start playing, I wish I would've proposed that the teams be guys versus girls, so I could've stood next to Cat. As it is, she's a good twenty feet away next to the other board and Cassie.

Regardless, the game is fun. I adore watching Cat get excited when her toss lands us a point. Even in heels, she has a decent throw. I'm guessing she didn't play many sports growing up, given the fact that her modeling career started so early on, but I bet she would've been good at them if she had. Which is something I'd talk to her about if she were standing next to me.

Instead, I have Asher cheering on himself. His competitive side comes out as it always does, but it doesn't bother me. I'm too busy staring at Cat and admiring how incredibly beautiful she is to worry about beating his ass.

"Game point," Asher says before tossing his bean bag and landing it in the center hole of the board.

"Congrats." I hit him on the back and jog over to Cat.

"That was fun." She grins. "Asher loves to win, no?"

"Oh, yeah. Normally, I try a little harder. It's fun to see his face get all red as he plays, but I just wanted to get over here to you. You were so far away." I stand before her, rocking back and forth between my legs, like a nervous boy in front of a goddess—which is pretty factual.

She blows out a laugh. "Oh, stop. You act as if you can't be away from me for longer than a couple of seconds."

"I mean...I can. But I don't like it." I extend my hand. "Are you hungry?"

She peers down at my outstretched arm, and for a moment, I think she's going to blow me off, but she slides her fingers through mine. "Yeah, I am."

"Alright. Then let's get you something to eat." I lead her across the grass and up to the wooden deck where

Amos and Alma's mother have laid out a smorgasbord of food.

We fill our plates and sit next to our friends. Quinn is telling everyone about the close encounter she had with a stingray while Ollie just shakes his head with an adoring smile on his face. Hanging out together like this —Cat and me with our mutual friends—is nice. I could see us together like this in the future. It just works.

It's a good day, and it gives me hope that at the end of this, everything will work out just fine.

CHAPTER 22

CAT

I haven't seen Everett today, and it's weird. He's sent me a few texts saying he was thinking about Benny and me, but that's it. No flower deliveries or romantically themed texts. No takeout from an incredible restaurant showed up on the doorstep. After two weeks of his constant affection, the void of his adoration is crushing. And I'm not sure how I feel about that.

It's silly, but I feel as if I'm betraying myself just in the fact that I miss him. It's come to the point where craving a man makes me feel weak. My ex really did a number on me.

Logically, I know that Everett isn't Stephen. God—

he's nowhere close. Nonetheless, all of these emotions that have come to the surface over the past two weeks cause a panic within my gut because I remember the last time I felt like this and where it led me.

Ten years of loneliness and regret isn't easily forgettable.

I rushed into my relationship with Stephen thinking it was true love, a case of love at first sight. I won't make that mistake again.

Yet the fact remains…I miss Everett.

I Velcro the side of Benny's diaper. "What's your daddy up to today?" I smile down at my little cherub.

Regardless of what happens between Everett and me, Benny will now know her father, and that's amazing. Every child deserves to know where they come from.

"Cat!" Alma calls from the foyer.

I finish pulling Benny's cute little bloomers over her diaper and pull down her cotton sundress. "What does your auntie want?" I ask my daughter. Leaning in, I kiss her cheek.

"One second." I position Benny in the middle of the blanket on the floor and place her turtle rattle in her hand. "I'll be right back."

Hopping up from the floor, I meet Alma in the foyer, where a huge box wrapped in silvery glitter paper and an enormous pink silk bow rests on the tile at her feet.

"What's that?" I ask.

"A delivery…for you." A knowing smile spreads across her face, and I squint in her direction.

I open my mouth to question her, but before the words come out, she's walked away, leaving me alone with the giant box.

I guess we'll see what he's been up to after all.

When I pull on the ends of the bow, it unravels and glides to the ground. The paper is so pretty. I hate to rip it, but anticipation gets the better of me, and I tear into it.

A gasp escapes my lips when I pull the lid from the box. It's filled with what must be hundreds of beautiful white daisies.

As I move some of the flowers to the side, an edge of a smaller box is visible. I start picking up handfuls of daisies and place them in the lid of the box on the floor. I remove most of the flower confetti until the box's contents are visible.

My heart beats rapidly, and I pull in a deep breath, willing the tears filling my eyes to stay away.

It's our beginning.

There's a gift-wrapped package of martini glasses, and I think back to the first drink we shared together at the casino bar. An MGM Casino plastic bucket is to the side of the glasses, filled with slot machine tokens. There's a mini-roulette wheel with a set of pink and blue chips, the color we each chose during that first roulette game…where we had our first kiss.

"No way." I shake my head and reach into the gift shop bag, pulling out the identical gaudy sports pieces he dared me to wear that day—a gray Piston's basketball T-shirt, orange Detroit Tiger's sweatpants, and a blue Lion's ball cap.

They're all new, with tags, unlike the set I wear to bed back at home.

He remembered every detail.

My brows furrow when I stop to take in the unfamiliar pieces, a new breast pump and a set of bottles. Before I can ponder those additions, I pick up the notecard addressed to Daisy.

My Daisy Hotlips,

When I first saw you sitting at the casino bar, sad and alone, I knew I had to cheer you up. Buying you that drink and initiating our game was the best thing I've ever done. I remember everything about our first day together because, truthfully, it was the best day of my life. Every moment was perfection.

You have one full day left here. Give it to me. Please.

Alma is set to watch Benny for the day. There's a pump and bottles to prepare. I even got you an outfit to wear. ;-)

Spend your last day here with me as we did a year ago. We'll play our game with a few modifications.

. . .

Rule 1: *Only speak in ~~lies~~ truths.*
   Rule 2: *~~One day only~~. The start of something incredible.*
   Rule 3: *Have fun. (No changes needed)*
   Rule 4: *Promise you ~~won't~~ will fall in love with me.*

I'll pick *you up in the morning.*

Love,
   Your Bernard Peppercakes

I hold the note to my chest, only now noticing the tears rolling down my cheeks. I can't do that. I can't leave Benny for a day and recreate something that...I don't know if I even want to recreate. It's a lot. Pressure builds in my chest as my anxiety grows. All the scenarios and questions are pinging around in my head. Dueling emotions run rampant in my mind as the doubt pushes against excitement, and worry battles hope, but the one that screams the loudest is fear.

I'm afraid.

I'm terrified of rule number four.

Rule number four could crush me. I can't allow it because it's not just me anymore. I must be strong for Benny now. I can't risk it.

"You should go," Alma urges from behind me.

I turn to face her, swiping my hands under my eyes to dry the tears. I shake my head. "I don't know."

"Love is terrifying, Cat. It's a leap of faith, and sometimes a scary one. I know you're confused and not sure what to think right now, but you'll never know if you don't try. The only way to fall in love is to be vulnerable." She extends a hand and pulls me up.

I circle my arms around her. She hugs me back.

"I don't want to make another mistake."

"Who's to say he'll be one? You have to stop comparing everyone to Stephen. It's not fair. Plus, you could be missing out on the love of your life." Alma squeezes my arms and takes a step back.

"But I already have her."

Alma grins. "Your heart has room for more. Trust me."

I look down at the box of goodies.

"You don't have to make any huge decisions right now. Just agree to one day and see where it goes," she suggests.

"One day can change a lot." I chuckle. "My one day is in there shaking a rattle right now."

"See how good that day turned out for you?" Alma raises a brow.

"And you're okay watching her?" I ask.

"Are you kidding? We'll have a blast. Between me, Amos, Love, and my mom…she'll never be put down.

It'll be great. You know I've done the baby thing before. I can handle it."

Reaching for a Daisy, I say, "I'm not worried about that. It's everything else. Plus, I've never spent an entire day without her."

"It'll be fine," she reassures me again.

"Okay." I sigh…relenting.

"Yay! Okay." Alma reaches into the box and grabs the breast pump and package of bottles. "I'm going to get these washed real quick. You need to drink lots of water so you can pump a bunch tonight."

"Sounds fun." I scoff.

She scrunches her nose. "Oh, it's a joy alright."

Alma practically skips to the kitchen with the pump and bottles in hand.

If anyone knows what it's like to have their heart broken, it's her, yet she still loves fiercely. I remember giving her similar advice to that in which she just gave me years ago. It seemed as clear as day when I was the one giving advice instead of the one being vulnerable. Yet the logic is the same. I'll never know if I don't try.

Holding the daisy in my hand, I pull off a white satin petal. "He loves me."

Releasing the lone petal, it falls to the floor, and I pull another. "He loves me not."

I repeat the pattern until a single petal is left attached. I squeeze it between my finger and thumb and pull it from the yellow middle. With a sigh, I say, "He loves me."

I watch the final petal fall and release a small chuckle. "I guess we'll see."

CHAPTER 23

EVERETT

Standing beside my car, I can't contain my smile when she exits Alma's front door in a tight little black dress and strappy black heels. Her brunette hair cascades over her bare shoulders in waves. She's the most beautiful sight I've ever seen. Utterly gorgeous.

"Oh, come on! Where's the outfit?" I protest though I knew damn well she wouldn't wear it.

She shakes her head. "No way was I wearing that out in public again."

"Aw…but you were so cute in it last time." I step forward to meet her.

"I'm cute in everything," she quips. "But there was no

chance in hell I was going to spend my day gallivanting around in mismatching sweats again."

I scan her glorious body. "No bag?"

She bites her bottom lip. "I packed one." She seems hesitant. "I didn't know…"

"Where is it? Let's bring it, just in case. Better to have it and not need it than the other way. It's not a commitment to anything. Okay?"

"Okay." She nods. "It's just inside the door, in the foyer."

I jog toward Alma's entry door.

It opens as I reach for the handle. "Hey." Alma greets me. She holds Bernadette in her arms.

"Hey, Benny girl." I kiss her head.

Alma nods toward the bag. "Don't let her see the baby. She'll never leave."

"It was a hard morning for her?" I question.

"Yeah, it's always hard to leave, but it will be good for you both to figure things out. You two have fun." She raises her brows with a grin, causing me to laugh.

"That's the plan." I grab the leather handles of the bag. "Bye, baby." I wave to Benny and thank Alma before shutting the front door before Cat catches a glimpse of our daughter.

I saunter back to the car and open the passenger door for Cat and toss the bag in the back seat before running around the front and getting in the driver's side door.

"Thank you for agreeing to this," I say in all sincerity. "I know it was hard for you to leave today. I get that you're nervous about making a mistake. Thank you for giving me a chance."

Clicking in her seat belt, Cat nods and smooths her hands over her dress-clad thighs.

With a sigh, she says, "Let's do this, Bernard."

"You got it, Daisy."

* * *

Just being here with Cat brings back so many emotions. If there really is such thing as a perfect day, it's the day we spent together a year ago in this casino.

I thread my fingers through hers and lead her through the grand entryway.

"Feels weird and incredible at the same time. Doesn't it?" I ask.

She nods. "Exactly. It's like it was yesterday but at the same time, so much as happened since that day."

"It sure has. So where should we start?" I quirk a brow.

"Obviously, we need to begin with a martini." She grins, squeezing my hand.

"My thoughts exactly."

She leans into my arm as we make our way back to the bar where we first met. Feeling her warmth beside me, her hand in mine stirs all sorts of emotions. I have high hopes for today. It's my last shot to "win" her over. She's leaving tomorrow and taking my daughter with her.

I need her to see what I see and feel what I feel. Our future seems so clear to me, vividly so, yet she still has doubts. Today, I hope to erase each and every one.

We order our beverages and make small talk.

Our drinks are set before us. Cat holds the stem and lifts her martini toward mine. "What are we toasting to?"

"The future," I say.

She clinks her glass against mine. "To the future. So what game are we playing today?"

I shake my head. "No games today. The future can only be built on reality, right?"

Her face falls ever so slightly, and she looks mildly disappointed. I chuckle. "I didn't say we weren't going to have fun. But no lies today. It's your last day here, and I want you to hear everything I'm feeling, and I want to hear the same from you."

"That makes sense." She grins, taking another sip of her drink.

"Except there are a few things, not really game-related, per se, but aspects of last time that we should definitely do." I turn toward her.

"Like?"

"Like kissing. A lot."

She covers her mouth and laughs. "Oh my gosh, Everett."

"What?" I shrug. "I'm just being honest."

"Fine," she says.

"Fine?" I laugh. "Just like that? What about your no-touching rule?"

She pulls her bottom lip into her mouth, and the slight nibble has me all sorts of horny.

"I don't know. In the spirit of honesty, I want it, too. Maybe it's this place or nostalgia or whatever, but… yeah." She grins. "Kisses would be welcome."

No additional invitation needed so I cup her cheeks between my hands and pull her face toward mine. I have wanted to kiss her a thousand times over the past week and a half, and I knew she wanted it too.

She's had fortress-sized walls up since the lake, and despite my charm and our mutual desire, her guard has been impenetrable. She has this idea that she has to be so strong for our daughter, so she doesn't make any mistakes.

Yet I'm not a mistake. Cat and I together are not a mistake. We're fucking destiny.

This right here—a chance—is exactly what we need. I knew this place could give it to us. The nostalgia-soaked memories are powerful and performed beautifully—evaporating her walls. Just like that.

The kiss is desperate and deep. Our tongues dance to the symphony of our lust-filled breaths. It's entirely inappropriate for the public eye, but I couldn't care less. My mouth is on hers, and that's where it's going to stay.

Everything else fades away—the bartender, the other patrons, the dings of the slot machines, and music coming from the wall speakers. It's just Cat. Me. And our incredibly matched mouths. How can one woman be so perfect for me?

She abruptly plants her hand against my chest and pushes me away.

"Wait." She gasps.

"What?"

Her lips are red and swollen from kissing, and I need them. Right now. On me.

"We have to…We can't…" She sighs.

"Oh, I think we can." I lean in.

She chuckles. "Be serious."

"I'm completely serious."

"We can't just do it right here on the barstool," she argues. "We need to chill."

"Um…" I feign discomfort. "I didn't say anything about doing it. I thought we were just kissing."

She drops her chin to her chest and huffs out a laugh. "You know what I mean. We have to slow down, or we will be doing it on the barstool. You and I, we're too…"

She struggles to find the right word, and I answer for her. "Perfect together."

"Compatible," she answers.

"There's no such thing as too compatible." I raise my

hand and drag my thumb down her beautifully plump lip.

She scrunches her nose and gently bites my thumb. I pull my hand away.

"You know what I mean. If you want to use this day to figure some things out, we'll need to come up for air once in a while. Plus, what we were just doing would take us straight to a hotel room."

I raise a brow. "So there's going to be a hotel room?"

Her cheeks blush. "That's not what I'm saying."

Pouting my lips, I tilt my head to the side. "No, I think it was."

"Everett." She giggles and hits my chest. "Stop."

I lift my hands in surrender. "I'm just saying, if you want me to get us a hotel room, I'm cool with it." I raise my voice a little louder. "You don't have to beg me to sleep with you, okay?"

Cat covers my mouth with her hand and looks around the space. "Oh my gosh, stop!" she whisper-hisses.

I laugh, and she drops her hand.

"I just wanted you to hear me. I'm open to whatever the day brings."

She rolls her eyes. "No, you wanted the whole bar to hear you."

"No. Just you. But if they all know you're taken, that's fine with me, too."

She finishes her martini and sets the glass down. "So, what's first on the agenda?"

I raise my hand to catch the bartender's attention and order two more drinks.

"I was thinking shopping…but you really won't wear the outfit?"

"God, no." Her sweet facial features morph into a look of complete disgust, and I can't help but laugh.

"Fine." I scoff. "But you're so cute in them."

"Well then…good thing you have your memories from last year to hold you over because I won't be donning that atrocious outfit in public again," she says before whispering something under her breath.

"Hey, that's not fair. What was that last part?"

"Nothing." She feigns innocence.

"Tell me."

She releases a sigh. "I said, only at night."

"Only at night?" I quirk a brow in question.

She presses her lips together. "Yes. I wear the sweats from last year to bed…most nights…unless they're dirty."

"Seriously? I have to see this."

She shrugs with a sheepish grin. "I left them back home."

"Hmm. I'll just have to imagine you wearing them, I suppose. I have to say, I think it's awesome that you wear them every night. It makes me happy."

She lifts her shoulders. "They're comfortable."

"They also make you feel closer to me. Making you think about me. Right?"

Cat's beautiful greens catch my stare and hold me in their spell. "Since we've sworn to tell the truth tonight… there hasn't been a day in the past year that I haven't thought about you."

Her declaration causes a small puff of air to escape my lungs and I look at her with wonder. "Same," I admit. "Same."

CHAPTER 24

CAT

I should be embarrassed. Everett straddles me from behind on the casino stool and kisses my neck as I place pink chips on the roulette table. It takes everything in me to concentrate on my bets and not his mouth against my skin.

How can someone's lips be so freaking magical?

We've taken PDA to a whole new level, a should-be-ashamed level. But still…I don't care. I need him. To kiss me. Touch me. Love me.

As much as he can because today's my last day here.

It's now or never.

I've attempted to be responsible over the past two weeks and have tried to get to know him on a deep and personal level. At this moment, I'm questioning my life choices. Why did I wait? Now, today is all I have, and the thought makes me feel sick. I should've allowed myself to enjoy every bit of him while I could.

My home is so far away. God...I'm going to miss him. So. Much.

This place brings back so many memories. Just over a year ago, in this same location, was one of the best days of my life even though it started out as one of the worst. That's the Everett effect. He can take anything and make it good. Because he's so wonderful.

He truly is.

While today has the same air as last year, it's so much different. It's not two strangers drunkenly galloping around in a web of lies and laughter. It's a partnership that created someone beautiful, who've been reunited against all odds, and who've crammed a lifetime of getting to know one another into fourteen days.

We're so much more than strangers. We're connected—through our daughter—for life. Regardless of where this day may lead us, I will always have Everett, and he will always have me as we learn to navigate parenthood together.

If I'm honest with myself. I don't want a replay of last year—as fun as it was. I'm not the same person as I was then, and I'm glad for it. What I needed that day and what I need now are utterly different.

Everett said today is about truth, so I need to give

voice to mine.

The dealer calls a number and starts clearing the losing chips before he pays the winners. I stand from the stool and hold my hand out to Everett.

"Let's go." I pull on his hand.

"But you won!" He raises a brow and looks toward the roulette table.

"I don't care. I need to get out of here. Let's get a room." I pull in a deep breath as my chest rises and falls with anticipation of what's to come.

Everett's mouth falls open, and he nods in understanding. "Okay. I hear ya." He taps the table near our chips, alerting the dealer to the fact that we want to check out.

The dealer trades my stacks of pink chips for the ones we turn in for money, and Everett snatches them up.

He holds them out before me. "These here…will get us a suite." He winks and threads his fingers through mine as we head toward the cashier.

A couple of transactions later and we've cashed in our chips and have purchased a suite for the night. Unlike last year when we spent an entire day in the casino before going to the room, today we lasted an hour.

His arms push against the walls of the elevator, boxing me in on either side, as he leans in to kiss me.

"We gave downstairs a valiant effort," he says against

my lips.

I lift my arms and thread it through the short hair at the nape of his neck. "We really did. Almost an hour." I sigh as his tongue enters my mouth.

He presses his body against mine as the elevator ascends toward one of the top floors. I can feel his hard desire against my stomach, and it's intoxicating.

"Everett." I whimper as I ride his thigh between my legs.

"We're almost there." He groans, biting my bottom lip.

The elevator doors ding open, and he steps back, taking my hand in his, and pulls me into the hallway. We practically sprint to our room.

The second the hotel room door closes behind us we're undressing as quickly as humanly possible.

"I want to go slow and taste every bit of you, but first…I need…" Everett moans through labored breaths, pushing my bare back against the hard wooden door.

"Me too." Is all I can say before he pushes my knee up and to the side, and thrusts into me in one hard motion.

I cry out as he hits deep. A mixture of pain and pleasure sting every one of my nerves and the sensation burns me from my head to my toes. "Oh, my God…" tears fill my eyes as he pounds into me relentlessly against the door. It's so good, it's hard to take the sensations coursing through me. I needed this more than I realized, and I can tell that Everett did, too.

The sex is carnal—two souls desperate for connection.

The lust-filled air is saturated with intense moans, and the rhythmic thud of my back against the door. It's more than sex—it's necessity.

I scream out as the sensations build. My body begins to shake, and the orgasm hits me intensely hard. I close my eyes and revel in the feeling. Everett picks up speed as he chases his release, a satisfied growl escapes as he empties inside me.

Our bodies are sweaty and limp as he picks me up and carries me to the bed where we both fall with an exhausted exhale.

"Fuck me!" Everett moans with a satisfied sigh.

"Indeed!" I close my eyes and feel the aftermath of the waves of my orgasm vibrate through my muscles.

"Sorry, that was such pent-up desperation. I'll do better," he says.

I smile lazily. "You can try but that was pretty incredible."

"We should pace ourselves." He states.

"You think?" my voice skeptical.

"I mean, right? We have all day, and a jacuzzi tub which we'll need to use. Food service will be ordered. It will be a whole experience. We can't be falling asleep at noon."

I chuckle weakly. "I don't know. Going hard and fast until we pass out from exhaustion is tempting."

"This is your fault, you know? Your no touching rule. Now, we're all desperate and sex deprived."

I turn over on my side and prop my arm under my head. "I like desperate sex."

He turns to face me and supplies the sexiest smile. "I like all sex, with you. Slow, fast, desperate…exhausted. I'll take it all."

"We are pretty compatible in that department," I admit with a lazy grin.

"Oh fuck!" his eyes go wide. "I forgot a condom. I never forget…oh no…I was so caught up…"

"Hey." I reach out and cup his cheek. "It's okay. I'm nursing. No pregnancy here. And, I haven't slept with anyone since you…so…"

"Are you sure? I feel like such a dick. I can't believe I didn't stop and think about that. I thought that whole can't get pregnant while nursing thing wasn't real?"

"No, it's pretty real. I suppose there are exceptions, but I think we're good, especially since she's still so young and exclusively nursing. I think it can be an issue later down the line when the baby is weaning and eating other foods."

"Okay, if, you're sure. I've been tested many times and never forget to use a condom…usually." He scrunches his face in an apology.

"It's fine. We're good." I reassure him.

"Maybe that's why it was so incredible. Huh? There wasn't a barrier between us."

I press my fingers against his full lips. "Could be. I just think it was because it was us, and it's been so long."

"Yeah, you're right. That's what it is." He reaches over and wraps his arm around my waist, pulling me against him.

He kisses me, slow and sweet. The desperation is absent now as his mouth cherishes mine, and it's everything.

"Have you ever done it in a jacuzzi bathtub?" he asks between kisses.

"No," I say, not completely honest. I actually have but he loves when I experience firsts, and his satisfied smile is worth a little white lie.

"Then I'm…"

Kiss.

"Going…"

Kiss.

"To run…"

Kiss.

"You…"

More kisses.

"A bath!" He pulls my face into his for one long kiss that ends with a smacking sound.

I giggle. "Okay, you do that."

The momentary absence of his soft skin against mine leaves me feeling desperate, and alone. I start to think about my decision. I must decide. Or maybe I don't. I could think about it for a while. Yet the truth is, leaving here with any answer besides yes will crush him, I know it.

I wiggle my head back and forth, pushing all my thoughts away. Nope. Today is about connecting. I need him as much as he needs me…and that, for today, is enough.

The decision will come tomorrow.

"Get your naked ass in here, Hot Stuff!" Everett calls from the bathroom.

"Coming." I giggle and stand from the bed.

Steam fogs the mirrors, and a faint smell of lavender fills the air.

"I used the hotel's shampoo as bubble bath," he says from inside the tub where he waits for me in bubbly water.

I climb into the water.

"I have a spot for you, right here." He motions toward his lap.

I bite my lip and slide down onto his hard length with a heated moan.

"Perfect." He exhales grabbing my hips.

Resting my elbows on his shoulders, I stay still allowing him to fill me completely as his stare holds mine.

"You are so beautiful." He raises an arm from the water and tucks my hair behind my ears.

Sitting forward he trails soft kisses over my collarbone and down my arm until he's kissing each finger.

"Every. Single. Part." He peppers kisses back up my arm and to my neck.

I close my eyes with an audible sigh as he takes my earlobe between his lips.

He leans back and squeezes my breasts in his palms. "What I would do with this body if I had access to it every day." He closes his mouth around my nipple and flicks it with his tongue.

A rush of need explodes between my legs, and I need to move.

I grab onto the ceramic tub behind him and lift myself up before I fall back down, water sloshing up the sides of the tub.

Everett sits back and grasps my waist. His lids are heavy with lust as he watches me move. His tongue peeks out, licking his bottom lip before he pulls it into his mouth with his teeth. He's so incredibly sexy and it makes the chase for release that much more pressing. I pick up speed.

His mouth is parted as he breaths heavily, guiding my movements with his hold on my hips.

"Oh, fuck…Cat…I've never…you…" his eyes close as he voices his pleasure in broken gasps.

I've made love. Had sex. Fucked before. But this… with Everett is something else entirely. I've never felt this way. So in tune. Connected. When he's inside me, I want to give him everything.

The room is filled with heated groans and the sound

of water splashing as I move harder and faster atop him.

Our orgasms hit hard, and we cry out in unison as our bodies shake with ecstasy.

I fall against his chest, and he draws lazy circles over my back as we pull in long, deep breaths.

"Two down. How many more to go?" He kisses the top of my head.

I plant small kisses across his chest. "I don't know. How many more you got in you?"

"With you? Who knows? You do something to me that makes it hard to stop."

I sit up to take him in and his eyes go wide. "Geez, Cat. Your boobs are huge."

I throw my head back and laugh. "Yeah, they're really full. The pump is in the car."

"Are they painful when they're that full?"

"A little bit, yeah. I don't want to go to the car, though."

"Me either but I also don't want you to be in pain."

"I can manually express them." I squeeze the skin of my breast toward my nipple and milk squirts out.

Everett's eyes get bigger, and he pushes back toward the rear of the tub. "Holy shit."

I laugh some more. "What? Is this a first for you?"

He nods wildly. "Um, yes. Definitely never seen this before. You are the first nursing mother I've been with."

"That's probably a good thing."

"I'd say so." He tilts his head and watches in fascination as I express some more milk, relieving some of the pressure in my breasts. "Will you think poorly of me if I admit that I'm oddly turned on right now?"

"No." I shake my head with a giggle.

We stay in the tub for a while longer and Everett washes every inch of me with a soapy cloth, and I return the favor. When the water runs cold, we get out and dry off before putting the hotel robes on and climbing into bed.

"I could get used to this you know?" he says.

"What? Me in a bathrobe?"

"No, touching and kissing you whenever I want."

"Me, too." I reach over and move a lock of his hair from his forehead. He's so handsome and so good. It's crazy to me that he hasn't been snatched up already. "Why are you still single?"

He leans back, his brows furrowed. "What?" He scoffs.

"I'm serious. You're such a great guy, and you're handsome. I don't know why you're not already committed."

He circles his arms around my bare waist and pulls me closer, a content smile on his face. "I've never met anyone I wanted to be serious with."

"Really? I find that hard to believe. No one?"

He shakes his head. "No one. I don't know why. For a while, I thought I was flawed somehow…like in my thinking or with relationships. But now, I realize it's because I was waiting for you. My heart knew not to waste time with others because it could open for you. There's no one else for me. We're it—you and me. There's not a doubt in my mind."

"Not a single one?"

"Nope." He leans in, his lips pressing against my own ever so softly in a whisper of a kiss. "I've been waiting for you my whole life, Caterina."

Our kiss deepens. His hands move across my body with expert precision until we're making love once more. I feel safe and whole, but most of all, I feel loved when I'm with Everett.

The rest of the day is spent in bed, and it's glorious. We order room service—eating, laughing, and chatting over silver food trays. We explore each other's bodies, and he gives me more pleasure than I've ever known. Every moment is incredible, and I'll remember this day forever. It's the perfect goodbye.

We come together for a final time; our bodies connect as if they were made to do so. Sated and happy, he pulls me against him, and I snuggle into his chest, wanting every inch of his skin against mine as sleep pulls me under.

"I love you." The honest declaration falls from my lips.

His breath is shaky. "I love you, Cat."

Regardless of what tomorrow brings, I'm eternally grateful we had today.

CHAPTER 25

EVERETT

The silky sheets smell like her perfume. It's intoxicating. I breathe in, a huge smile on my face, and my body starts to hum in remembrance of our night together.

Her words played on repeat in my dreams, *I love you.*

She loves me, and God, how I love her.

I adore everything about her. Obviously, she's stunning, which was, of course, the initial draw, but she's so much more than beautiful. She's good, and kind, and fun. She's literally the woman I've always wanted but thought was too good to be true. She's my dream. My destiny.

Most importantly, she's a great mother. When I think

of our life together and our children—there's only happiness. We work. Our life is going to be incredible.

I'm eternally grateful to the casino gods that brought us together initially. And, again last night, I reminded her—because let's face it, I already knew—that together we're fire. Unstoppable. Perfection.

My heart stutters when I reach my arm out and don't feel her. I force my sleepy eyes open and look around the room for her. She's nowhere in sight.

"Cat," I call out, hoping she's in the bathroom.

It's then that I notice the note on the desk.

"You've got to be kidding me." I groan and jump from the bed.

Snatching up the note, I read the contents.

BERNARD,

THANK YOU FOR YESTERDAY. It was perfect in every way.

You...are perfect in every way.

Unfortunately, I'm still lost.

There are so many unanswered questions swirling in my head.

I can't make a life-altering decision with so much uncertainty.

You are the father of my daughter, and for that reason alone, you will always be in my life.

I wasn't lying when I said I love you. I do.

But sometimes, love just isn't enough.

I'll be in touch, and we'll figure out a visitation schedule that works for us both.

I'm so glad the universe brought us together again.

Benny's life will be fuller with you in it.

Until we meet again.

Daisy

"Fuck, no!" I growl.

I'm not sure what I feel as I get dressed at rapid speed. Anger? Disappointment? Hurt? It's all there in one way or another.

I don't know what else I can do to prove to Cat that she and I are endgame.

It's clear as day to me. The universe brought us together—twice—for a reason. It's not coincidence. There are no two people on this earth more suited for each other than the two of us.

I get that she has baggage. But don't we all?

What's the point of overcoming life's obstacles if you're not going to go after what you want in the end? She wants me—us. There's no doubt in my mind. She's just afraid. I'm still not clear as to what she's so terrified of. I'm nothing like her ex, and she knows that. I've tried to prove myself and my intentions in every way I can. I've promised her everything because the truth is, she can have it all.

I just want her and our daughter. I want to start living as the family we're meant to be.

Before stepping out of the hotel, I brush my teeth. Morning breath isn't going to put a damper on our magical kiss—the one after she agrees to spend the rest of our days together. Maybe that's the problem. I've been letting her call the shots. She's dictated everything, but she's clearly confused.

It's time I tell her how it's going to be. Because—God—she must know, in her heart, that we're meant to be.

* * *

I TIGHTEN my grasp on the steering wheel until my knuckles ache. The cadence of my heart accelerates as signs for the airport come into view.

If I had eaten anything this morning, I would've lost it when Alma told me that Cat and Benny had already left for the airport. Sick doesn't even describe that blow. Utterly nauseating.

She left.

She snuck out of the hotel, got a ride back to Ann Arbor, picked up our daughter, and bolted to the airport. Not only did she leave me but she also took Benny without letting me say goodbye.

I'm furious. I want to scream and...break things. This is so un-fucking-fair.

I bite the inside of my cheek to keep the tears away. I'm not a crier. I'm not my brokenhearted mother begging to be loved.

Not a chance.

I'm a good person and a great father. I'm not going to beg anyone to love me. Fuck that.

I tried so hard to get Cat to see us the way I do, but she doesn't. Her actions today prove that she can't. What am I going to do with that? Nothing. There is absolutely nothing I can do. I can't make her love me.

But I will be damned if she's going to take my daughter to the other side of the earth without so much as a goodbye.

I park and race inside the airport. Thanks to Alma, I know that Cat is leaving from gate B-36. Scanning the large screen TVs with all the flight information, I see a flight to Orlando, Florida, leaving from gate B-25.

"Orlando it is."

I'm relieved when I approach the airline's ticket counter to find only one couple in line. At least something is working in my favor today.

"Can I have a one-way ticket to Orlando on the next flight, please?" I ask the older woman with a white bun atop her head.

"It's your lucky day. There is a seat available," she

says with a voice that has smoked way too many cigarettes. "Checking any bags?"

"No bags," I answer.

"License?"

I slide my license and credit card across the counter. She eyes me for a moment before returning her attention back to the computer screen. Her brightly colored red fingernails click against the keyboard.

"You a big fan of the mouse?" she asks with a gravelly voice.

"I'm sorry?"

"Mickey Mouse. Are you going to Disney?" she clarifies.

"Oh, no." I shake my head. "Going to see my baby momma."

She nods. "Ahh. I see." She retrieves a boarding pass from the small printer on the side of the computer screen and hands it to me, along with my license and credit card. "Well, here you go. Security is down to your left."

"Thank you," I say, taking the documents from her hand.

I bolt toward security as fast as possible without looking deranged. The last thing I need is a good ole security search to slow me down. Cat's flight leaves in an hour, so it will probably be boarding in thirty minutes.

Eyeing the line at security, I pull in a breath. *It's fine.*

It's fine. I shuffle back and forth on my feet, imagining the people in line moving quickly.

My friend Cassie always talks about manifestation. I can hear her now. "Visualize what you want to happen, and the universe will materialize it for you. Don't send negativity out into the world, or that's what will be sent back to you."

Truthfully, I only half listen when Cassie begins to wax philosophical. It's usually a lot of mumbo jumbo that is interrupting something—quite often a sporting event or TV show—that I'm in to. Nodding and agreeing tends to quiet her lesson sooner, and so that's what I do. Digging deep into the recesses of my mind, I attempt to recall her words because—let's face it—I need all the help I can get.

I imagine the line moving at warp speed, and the smile on Cat's face when I get to her gate because she wanted me to chase after her. She'll cry happy tears when I ask her to stay…

"Boarding pass and license," a gruff voice orders, breaking my visualization, but it's cool. So far, so good—the line is moving quicker than it ever has. I think.

This is going to work.

Once I'm through the metal detector, I snatch my tennis shoes and wallet from the X-ray machine belt. Shoving my feet into the shoes, I search for the gate numbers.

"Gates twenty through forty to the right." I read the sign aloud. "Got it."

I'm approaching gate 36 in a matter of seconds, and I can finally pull in a deep breath when I see the passengers still seated in the waiting area.

I made it.

It doesn't take me long to find her. She sits along the back wall, by the floor-to-ceiling windows. Benny rests in her lap as Cat shoves a packet of wipes into her oversized purse.

Cat kisses the top of Benny's head, and my chest aches with a torrent of emotions. This is it. This is literally my last chance.

I chew on my bottom lip as I come up with the perfect words to say, and it's then that Cat lifts her face, her gaze catching mine. Her eyes go wide and, if I'm not mistaken, cloud with guilt. Or maybe I just hope it's guilt.

She props Benny against her hip and slides her bag onto her shoulder before standing.

I'm unable to move as she closes the distance between us. Anger, love, and pure desperation duel it out—bouncing on my heart.

She stands before me, a sad smile on her face.

I swallow the lump in my throat. "You left." The words come out in a hoarse whisper.

"I'm sorry. I–"

I cut her off. "That was really shitty, Cat."

"I know."

"You didn't even let me say goodbye." My eyes fill with tears, and I reach for my daughter.

I take Benny in my arms and hold her against my chest, kissing her soft head.

"Why are you doing this?" My words come out broken.

She presses her lips in a line and shakes her head. "I have to. I must go home."

"No, you don't. That's only been your home for the past year. You've been here for over half your life. I'm here, and I love you. We could be happy as a family. Don't tell me that you don't feel it…this insane connection. I know you do."

She closes her eyes and takes a deep breath before opening them again. "None of that matters."

"Of course, it matters," I growl. "It's everything. How can you say that?"

She wipes a stray tear that's rolling down her cheek. "Everett, I'm sorry. I am. It was cowardice to leave you like that this morning. I thought it might be easier, and I wanted our goodbye to be yesterday. It was selfish, I know, but I wanted to remember every incredible moment from yesterday when I thought of you. Not this —us fighting, and you hurt and angry. I didn't want this. I knew leaving would hurt you, but this is the only path for me right now. I figured after I left, we'd have space and time to really think about everything, and you would realize I was right."

"You're wrong, Cat. This is wrong. Leaving, taking Benny away, pretending that we're not fucking perfect together—all of it's wrong!" I plead.

A woman calls out section numbers on the speaker above us, causing Cat to still. "I'm sorry. That's us. We have to go. I know it doesn't seem okay right now, but I promise in time…it will be. You'll see Benny again. I'll be in touch."

Cat extends her arms. I pull Benny in for one more hug and press my lips to her head, inhaling the scent of her baby shampoo—committing everything about her to memory—before handing her back to her mother. My heart breaks at the realization that she'll have grown so much by the next time I see her in person.

The moment Cat takes my daughter from me, I'm overcome with intense anguish and a sorrow I've never felt. This is it. Seconds are all I have until they're gone.

My soul shatters as I do something I promised I'd never would.

Beg someone to love me.

"Please, Cat. I love you, and I know you love me. We can be happy, all of us. I know it. I feel it. We're not a mistake. We're destiny. The three of us…we're meant to be. I can make you happy, and I will. I'm not him. Believe that I'm not him," I beg.

She lifts her arm and cups my cheek with her hand.

"I know you're not him, Everett. You're so much more. I love you, too. I do. But as I said—it's just not enough. I'm sorry, but I must choose me."

"Cat." I hold her gaze in mine, her name a somber sigh, a final plea.

"I'm sorry." She shakes her head, her lips turned down before she turns and walks away.

She hands her boarding pass to the agent to scan and disappears down the jetway leading to the plane without so much as a glance back.

I watch her go with my child in her arms. What else can I do?

I fall back into a chair in the terminal, facing the window, and stare at the plane holding my entire life.

Completely numb.

I thought she'd stay. For the entire two weeks, I was confident she would. Surely, she'd never leave knowing how much I would love her.

I'm utterly exhausted after spending every minute trying to convince her to stay. I didn't mess up—not once. I put it all on the line, doing everything I could to prove that I was a chance worth taking and that our family was better together.

I couldn't have done more.

I made it clear that I chose her.

However, the problem is I can't make her choose me.

Now she's gone. And there's not a damn thing I can do about it.

CHAPTER 26

CAT

Buckled in tight, I hold my baby against my chest and take slow and deep breaths. It's not until the wheels leave the ground that the tears flow in torrential streams of heartache. My meltdown is sure to scare every other passenger in first class, but I don't care.

The plane ascends, pushing through fluffy white clouds. Tears stream down my face as I rock Benny in my arms. Her heavy eyelids put up a brief fight but succumb to the sleepiness of the hectic morning.

I secure her against me with my oversized scarf and hope she'll stay asleep for a while. My emotions are crashing into a dark place, and I need to pull myself out of it before she wakes.

Leaving Everett is the hardest thing I've ever had to do. Everything in me wanted to stay—to be his and to live the dream. A sliver of hope deep within me thought it was possible. *Possibly...*

A chance isn't enough.

I couldn't take that risk. I must do it right next time if there is a next time. Maybe I'm not cut out for love and marriage. My fated path could be raising my daughter, and if that's the case, I'm good.

Everything about the past two weeks was perfect. I don't doubt Everett or the fact that he thinks he loves me. He's a good person and will make an amazing father. I can see Benny spending her summers in Michigan—happy—with a dad who adores her. I believe I was meant to run into Everett again so my child could know him.

He's everything I think I want in a partner—kind, loving, funny, and sweet. He has a heart of gold and wears his emotions on his sleeve, and I love that about him. Yet I no longer trust my judgment. I've failed myself before, and I won't do it again, especially now that I have Benny. She deserves an absolute—a sure thing. Hell, so do I.

Happiness is worth more than a gamble.

Two wonderful weeks together, and a couple of magical—albeit *make-believe*—days at a casino, regardless of how incredible the physical attraction was, isn't enough of a foundation to build a life on.

"Excuse me, miss…" the flight attendant breaks into my thoughts, her voice hesitant. She holds out two white cotton towels, a warm wet one and a dry one.

I take them from her. "Thank you." My words are a broken whisper, and I force a smile before returning my stare out the window.

The soft clouds are below the plane, and the bright blue horizon extends as far as I can see. The world is so beautiful from up here. Heaven skies. It's so enchanting I could almost forget all the broken pieces of my soul. *Almost…*

I press the warm towel against my face in an attempt to wash away the heartbreak. I have so many people who love me, true friends and family, but at this moment, I feel so alone. I crave my person, the love of my life—my soul mate—the one who would protect me and love me no matter what. All the other connections are wonderful, but they're not the same as having a true partner in life.

The truth is, I've never had one. Once upon a time, I thought I would, but I was tricked.

There were moments with Everett these past two weeks when I thought he could be my one. But when I looked into what made him the man he is today, my confidence faltered. He grew up without a father watching his mother chase love.

He vowed from an early age that when he became a father, he would never leave. It's admirable of him and makes him a better man. I can't help but think that he desperately wants to be with me because we have a child together. It's noble and responsible, for sure. But that's not love—it's obligation.

I need a man who wants to be with me because he can't live without *me*.

If Benny wasn't here, would Everett still be fighting so hard?

No, I don't think he would.

The fact of the matter is that he left me in that hotel room a year ago. We had an incredible day and an amazing connection…and he left with just a note. Yes, that was always the plan. However, if I were his true soul mate, he wouldn't have left regardless of *the rules*. No matter how much I may want to—I can't let that go.

He didn't fight for me until there was a child involved, and I need a man to fight for me and choose me—no matter what. That's all there is to it.

I have no doubts that Everett could make me happy and love me…enough.

But I need more than that.

I need it all.

CHAPTER 27

EVERETT

"Dude. Come on. Get up. Get dressed. Join the living," Asher urges.

I ignore him and continue to stare at the TV. I blink, taking in what I'm watching, a Maury Povich talk show. What the hell? When did this start? Last I knew, I was watching...

What was I watching? I don't know.

I've been in a glazed-over daze, fueled by anger and heartbreak, but mainly rage.

The truth is, I have no idea how long I've been sitting here staring at the TV and wallowing in self-pity. The days have started to blur together. I do just enough not to get fired, and then I sit here and stew.

I fucking hate Cat for leaving.

Sigh.

That's a lie. I fucking love her.

But still…she left, and now…life just sucks.

I don't know what to do because the fact is I've never had my heart broken before. I think I've always avoided serious relationships, and now I know why. It blows. Loving someone and having her not love you in return is the absolute worst.

And…now I'm my mother. Unloved and unwanted.

I have worked my entire life to avoid this exact predicament. Yet I landed here just the same. I guess it was always meant to be. It's in my genes.

"Look. People are going to be arriving soon. A shower would be a good thing, man. It's all I ask. Just a shower," Asher says.

People? Here?

"What are you talking about?" I grumble.

"It's Saturday," he replies.

"It's Saturday?" I mimic, unable to believe an entire week has passed since she left.

Asher grabs the remote control from the arm of the couch and shuts off the TV. "Yes, it's Saturday. People are coming over…and soon. Come on, some socializing will do you good. Tannon, Jude, and the baby will stop by for a few minutes before everyone arrives."

Normally, having Tannon and her family stop by would leave me elated. I don't get to see her nearly as much as I'd like since she no longer lives across the hall. She's one of my best friends, and I miss her. Yet now, the thought of seeing her and her happy family…and baby… makes me feel ill.

"I don't know. Maybe I'll just chill in my room during the party." I sigh as I stand from the sofa, surprised at how much effort it took. *When was the last time I've eaten?*

"Nope. Get your ass in the shower. You're joining the living today," Asher says.

"You're fucking annoying," I grumble.

"Good. Now, go. They'll be here soon."

I stop in the kitchen and down a glass of water. I don't remember the last thing I've drunk, but if the cracks on my lips are any indication, it's been a while. "What's the theme?" I ask.

Asher and I have a music theme for every Saturday night party. It's always random, but it's always awesome.

"Well, since you were out of commission and didn't give me any input, I went with a guaranteed good time. We're doing an ode to Meatloaf," he says, sounding pleased with himself.

"Fuck that, Asher."

"What? You love Meatloaf." His tone surprised.

"Yeah, I do, and he's gone…like I need a reminder of all the shitty things in life." My voice is so melancholy that I'm starting to even hate myself.

"Okay. You're right. Too soon. How about a Swifty night? She just re-did all her old stuff."

"I'm over her, and actually, I'm starting to hate Taylor, if I'm honest…okay, that works."

Asher laughs. "Okay, Taylor Swift it is. You can wallow in your newfound hatred of her all night."

"Fine."

I retreat to my room and fumble through a shower, making sure to go through the necessary motions of brushing my teeth and putting on deodorant afterward. Break-up depression sucks.

When I exit my room, Tannon and her family, and Cassie are in the living room talking with Asher. Taylor Swift's song about a sweater plays quietly throughout the speaker, and I'm renewed in my newfound hatred of her. Who sings about a fucking sweater?

Truthfully, it feels good to direct my hate toward someone other than Cat.

"Hey!" Tannon stands and greets me with a hug.

"Hi," I offer.

She takes a step back, and for a moment, I forget my sadness because she looks so beautiful. Happiness is stunning on her.

"You look great, Tan." I smile.

"Thank you. I wish I could say the same for you." She cups my chin, pointing out the week of patchy stubble.

I shrug. "Eh, I'll get there."

"I'm sorry about Cat and everything. I really am."

"Thank you. It is what it is." I sigh.

Her husband, Jude, comes up beside her with their son, Eli, in his arms. Eli will be one in a couple of weeks, and I can't help wondering if I'm going to miss Benny's first birthday next year.

"Hey, buddy," I say to Eli, who gives me a goofy grin. "He's getting so big," I say to Tannon and Jude.

"I know. He's growing like crazy." Jude chuckles.

"We're heading over to Jude's abuelo's house for his niece's birthday, but I just wanted to stop by and see you all before your apartment fills with random drunk people." Tannon grins. "Life is so busy now, and we don't get to see you as much."

"I'm glad you did. I missed you." I take Eli in my arms. I bounce him up and down as he giggles. He's the perfect combination of both his mom and dad. Adorable. Like Benny is the perfect combination of Cat and me.

Ugh, I have to stop doing that. I have to stop inserting them into every thought, or I'm going to go crazy. "So tell me what Eli's new tricks are."

"He follows Lucifer around chanting cat, now," Tannon beams, referencing her black devil cat.

"Well, ca..." Jude chuckles.

"Close enough, but you should be teaching him to stay away from the crazy animal." I quirk a brow.

Tannon shakes her head. "No, Lucifer has calmed down now that he's a big brother. He's gotten better.

He's actually really sweet with the baby. He lets Eli pet his belly, and you know he doesn't allow anyone else to do that."

"Well, that's good, at least," I state.

"Eli can now walk and toss a ball at the same time," Jude adds.

I nod. "Nice. That takes skill. I can't even do that most days."

Holding Eli, I walk over to where Cassie and Asher are seated. I set him down on the ground to see how much his walking has improved.

"So glad you could shower for us," Cassie teases me.

"Well, Asher made me."

"Thank goodness for that." Cassie reaches over and squeezes my knee. "It'll get easier."

I know her words are meant to reassure me, but they don't. I don't want life without my daughter and Cat to get easier. It should always hurt because it's wrong. It's not how things are meant to be.

"So tell us everything." Tannon sits beside me. "We haven't spoken since Ollie and Quinn's wedding. Asher gave us some details, but I want to hear it from you."

I look at Asher. "You're such a gossip." I shoot him a glare, though there's no malice behind it.

"What? You were busy in Cat and Benny land, and your friends needed details." He shrugs.

I shake my head. "Oh, you love it…spilling all the tea."

"He does." Cassie chuckles. "He's a Chatty Cathy."

"Whatever." Asher rolls his eyes and looks at me. "Tell them yourself then."

I get them all up to speed on my mess of a life—filling them in on everything that's happened over the past several weeks. The more I talk, the more I want to say. It's oddly therapeutic to let it all out. I've spent the past week in such a dark place. Sharing with my friends lifts a weight off my chest.

The words fall from my lips as if I'm describing a scene in a movie—a romantic comedy gone wrong. From the outside looking in, my situation with Cat has all the makings of an epic romance—a one-night stand, a baby, another chance meeting, and then a two-week crescendo of heated tension that should ultimately end in the happily ever after. Yet there was no fairy-tale ending. Just me, chasing her through the airport, begging her to love me.

Pathetic.

Cassie and Tannon exchange a look, and although I can't quite make it out, pity is definitely involved.

"And, then she just got on the plane and left?" Tannon repeats the final sentence of my story.

I drop my chin to my chest. "Yep."

"Just like that?" Cassie presses her lips into a line.

"Just like that." I blow out a breath.

Tannon turns to Cassie. "I don't get it."

"Me either," Cassie replies.

"Me either," I chime in. "But it happened all the same. So now what?"

Cassie releases a sigh. "There has to be a reason."

"Yeah," Tannon agrees.

I turn to Tannon. "Well, what is it? You're the romance writer. What do I do in this situation?"

Tannon pulls her bottom lip into her mouth and bites the corner. "She's scared…" She nods slowly. "Okay, I got it." She looks at each of us. "She was in a horrible ten-year marriage, and because of that, she is wary about relationships. Right?"

"Right." Cassie nods.

"Well." Tannon looks at me. "I'm sure you told her about your daddy issues."

"What?" I protest.

"You know what I mean," Tannon says. "You were left by your dad, and you swore never to do that to your own child. So Cat shows up with your baby, and you immediately try to get her to fall for you. But…she questions whether you truly want to be with her or if it's just because you two have a child together. Having finally left her first husband, she doesn't want to settle for anything less than real love next time. She wants the fairy-tale ending."

"I tried to give it to her. She didn't want it," I say.

Tannon shakes her head. "She didn't *trust* it. She definitely wants it."

I frown. "Well, she doesn't want it from me."

"I don't believe that," Tannon says. "I think she does. From what you've said, you two have a great connection. You just have to make her believe it."

"I tried, Tan. I gave her everything I had. If she doesn't believe that I truly love her, I don't know what else to do."

Cassie pins me with her stare. "So if she showed up at Quinn's wedding without having had your child—just by herself—would you have wanted to be with her then?"

"Absolutely. You all know I couldn't stop talking about *Daisy the casino chick* for a solid six months. I mean, of course, I want to be in my daughter's life. But even without her, I'd still want to be with Cat."

"Then you gotta prove it to her," Tannon says. "Make Cat believe without a shadow of a doubt that she's the one and only person for you. You have to convince her that she's your destiny, soul mate, one and only—whatever you want to call it. She must truly believe it. And when she does—everything will be okay." With a smile, Tannon places her hand over mine and gives it a reassuring squeeze. "That's your storybook ending."

CHAPTER 28

CAT

"Say Mama." I lean in toward Bernadette and enunciate my name in dramatic fashion. "Ma-ma."

My cousin Anya laughs. "She's way too young to speak yet."

I shoot her a smile. "I know, but I'm going to make sure that her first word is my name."

Anya holds up a blue faux leather purse. "This line is gorgeous." She sets it on the display shelf beside the rest of the designer bags.

"I agree. Gorgeous." I scoop Benny into my arms and bounce her on my hip as I circle the space. She reaches her pudgy fingers out to touch the fabrics. "You're going to love clothes as much as your mama, aren't you?" I kiss her soft head.

With a content grin, I look around my store, and I'm happy. *I did this.*

A year ago, after officially retiring from modeling, getting a divorce, and moving home—I had no idea what I was going to do with the rest of my life. I couldn't be happier with my decision to open this boutique. It's just a short five-minute walk from my parents' restaurant, so I can see them whenever I want. I lucked out and scored an incredible location right in the center of Arbat Street in Moscow's shopping district. I hired my cousin Anya who was struggling after leaving an abusive relationship, and now she's thriving. The best part is I never have to be away from my daughter. My office in the back is a combo nursery-office-play room, and it has everything Benny or myself may require for a successful day at the shop.

I named my high-end boutique Prednaznachenny-*Destined*, in Russian. It seemed fitting. My path hasn't been easy, but every step of it led me here, and there's nowhere I'd rather be. I wouldn't trade any of it. I adore the people and experiences my journey has brought me. More than anything, I love being Bernadette's mother. I wouldn't wish a second of the years spent in my lonely marriage away because ultimately, it brought me to her.

The divorce, in that casino, led me to Everett. That incredible day made her…the love of my life.

I've been thinking about Everett since we left Michigan a month ago and going over everything he said to me. I know that he truly believes that a life with me is what he wants, but I don't think it is. He has this fantastical idea of what a family should be and how they should be together. It's noble of him, but it's not sustainable. I've been in a marriage where one of the people wasn't truly invested, and it was brutal. I refuse to let another marriage suffocate me. If I marry again, it will be because I am in love with a man just as much as he is in love with me.

Do I love Everett?

I can't pretend I don't.

Of course, I do.

He turned one of the worst days of my life into one of the best. He gave me Benny. He swept me off my feet for two weeks. But a lifetime is much longer. Having a child with someone doesn't mean I'm meant to be with him. It simply means, I'm meant to have my daughter.

I need the storybook ending, the true soul mate love. My fears have convinced me that Everett is more in love with the idea of being a father than he is a husband. He was fine leaving me in the one-night stand category until he found out about Benny.

I deserve to be cherished and adored. I'll wait for the right man.

Until then, I'll cherish myself and protect my heart. My daughter will have an amazing life—I'll make sure of it. She'll know and see her father because she should, and I owe that to her.

However, I owe myself, too. To the heart that loved fiercely without being loved in return, I'm owed a happily ever after. Maybe he's out there, or maybe he's not. Either way, I'm content in this life I've created.

"Where do you want me to put this shipment of new scarves?" Anya asks.

I set Benny down in her playpen with all her toys and make my way across the store to my cousin. "We have that scarf tree in the back. We could place it here." I point toward a shelf beside the purses. "Hanging them there. Don't you think?"

She nods in agreement. "Yeah, that would look nice."

I jerk my head toward the front of the store. "Do you hear that?"

"What?"

"The song. It's…" I listen, and my heart starts thumping forcefully within my chest. I shake my head. It can't be.

"Peter Gabriel." Anya chuckles. "'In Your Eyes.' I love this song. Remember how we used to watch…"

I hold out my hand to quiet her, then bring it to my trembling lips.

It can't be. He wouldn't.

On instinct and a prayer, I make my way to the front of the store. I want it to be him more than I knew was possible. I open the shop door, and a sob escapes my chest. I cover my mouth and blink away my falling tears.

There he stands, my Everett, on the stoned sidewalk of Arbat Street, a world away from Ann Arbor, Michigan, holding a large Bluetooth speaker over his head. At his feet is a large TV screen that's playing what appears to be a surveillance video of some sort. I step closer, and that's when I realize that the video is of him in the casino.

I gasp as more tears fall. He's in the hallway of the casino running from the elevator to the room door. But it isn't the suite's door. It's the hotel room I had last year. I recognize the clothes he's wearing from over a year ago. He desperately pounds against the door, and when I don't answer—because I was already gone—his face falls, chin to chest. He turns and leans against the hard surface, his shoulders slumped, as he slides to the ground. He rests his face in his hands, his entire body deflating with defeat.

The video loops back to the beginning, showing him running from the elevator again, and I look at him. In all reality, I haven't known this man before me for long, yet it feels like I've known him my whole life. It's as if I've loved him forever.

My heart beats for him, and everything in me wants to run to him, where I feel safe. In his arms is where I feel the most at peace. I couldn't admit it before. I was afraid to fail again. But it's glaringly obvious at this moment.

He's so beautiful it hurts. His hair is shorter and seems blonder in the afternoon sun. His bright hazels appear more green than brown today. His irresistible mouth turns up into a longing smile, and the dimple in his right cheek that I love so much makes an appearance.

"I went back," he finally says, lowering the speaker from above his head and setting it on the stoned walkway. "Last year when we were strangers on a one-day adventure. When we promised that there would be no truths. No strings attached. No feelings. I went back. You see, I left that Detroit casino and went home, only I couldn't quiet the feeling in my gut that I just walked away from the best thing that had ever happened to me. So I went back to beg you to stay and give us a chance. I barely knew you, yet I knew I didn't want to live without you. Before Benny, I fell for you. You— Caterina Avilova Araya—for you are enough. Were there no Benny, I'd still be here begging you to be mine. I love you. Hell, I think I've loved you from the moment I laid eyes on you."

I bring my hands to my face, covering my mouth as my lips quiver.

"I know you're scared," he continues. "But you don't have to be. No one on this earth will love you as much as

I do. I will literally do anything to make you happy. I just need you to give us a chance. A real chance."

"Okay." I nod through my tears.

"Okay?" He smiles wide. "Really?"

"Really," I say.

He steps toward me and circles his strong arms around my back, pulling me into his chest. His lips collide with mine, and it's better than my dreams—the ones I've been having of him since leaving Michigan. I thread my fingers through his soft hair as our tongues dance together. He's perfect. In his arms, I'm home.

We kiss until my lips turn numb, and my tears dry.

"That was perfect." I sigh. "Better than the movie."

"Hell yeah, it was better," he says. "For starters, it worked. You know I think nostalgia has clouded your judgment on that one."

"No way," I protest.

"Um, yes." He scoffs. "To be honest, the movie wasn't great. The guy was clearly in love with the chick, but she pushed him away for no reason. He did all these romantic gestures, including the boom box scene, and nothing. She ignored him until she had no one left." He leans in and plants a soft kiss against my lips. "Now, you, on the other hand…coming out crying, the gasps, the amazing kiss of a reunion—that's how she should've reacted in the movie."

I shrug. "Well, sometimes, girls need a moment to process and decide what they want."

He shakes his head. "All I'm saying is our version is so much better."

"Agreed." I wrap my arms around his neck and kiss him. It feels so good to have him this close again. "I can't believe you have that video."

"Yeah, I was thinking about how I could prove to you that Benny wasn't the only reason I wanted to be together. Then I remembered that I had gone back for you last year. Asher knows a guy who works for the casino security, so he pulled some strings and got me the video. Of course, the song over my head thing—I totally stole and did it better, might I add."

I laugh. "You did do it better. John Cusack is going to have to be okay with the fact that I've fallen in love with someone else."

"He better be okay with it because I'm never letting you go again. You're it for me, Cat. You're the love of my life. For always."

Another tear falls, and I bite my lip. "You're it for me, too," I agree. "This past month has been the worst. Thank you for coming here and fighting for me."

"I would do anything for you." He shakes his head. "Anything. Even moving to Russia."

"What? You're moving here?" I gasp.

"Don't you want me to?"

I take a step back. "I don't know."

"Well, I spoke to work, and all my tasks can be completed virtually. So I may have to get up in the middle of the night for an online meeting occasionally. But there's nothing I can't do here that I can there. As long as I have internet."

My heart melts for this man, and I cup his face in my hands. "You're the sweetest man in the world. But… Michigan is my home. I've spent my entire adult life there, and I miss it. I want to go back and raise our family there. If that works for you?" I raise a brow in question.

He blows out a sigh of relief. "Yes…that definitely works for me."

I can't help but laugh. "Good." I thread my fingers through his. "Well, come inside and see my store and Benny. She's missed you."

"I've missed you both more than you could know. I never want to know what a life without you is like again." He squeezes my hand in his.

"You'll never have to. I promise."

CHAPTER 29

EVERETT

Cat's family is exactly how I imagined they'd be —warm, nice, and just...good people. There are dozens of cousins, aunts, and uncles who have come out to her mother's restaurant to meet me. There's no way I'm going to be able to learn all their names and keep them all straight, but I'll certainly try.

I've never been to this part of the world, but I'm not disappointed. The food, culture, and people are all great. I love how Cat's mother and grandmother's restaurant took a piece of Spain and just plopped it into downtown Moscow.

"This is amazing, Mamá," I say to Cat's mom, who

insisted I call her mom now that I'm going to be a part of the family.

"I told you her paella was incredible," Cat beams, shooting a wink toward her mother. "She and Abuela are the best cooks."

I nod with a mouth full of paella. Once I swallow, I agree. "Absolutely. Delicious. Thank you so much."

"I'll teach you," Mamá says, patting my hand.

"I'd love that. Thank you."

"Everett made me several dinners, Mamá. He's a very good cook, too," Cat says.

I shake my head. "Not like this."

Cat and I decided to stay in Moscow for a couple of weeks to get her affairs in order. She's going to rent out her flat and keep her store. Her cousin Anya is going to stay on as manager and run the shop. Cat can order items and keep up with the paperwork from Michigan. It was important to Cat to keep the store for her cousin. She says Anya needs it. It's helped her become independent and leave an abusive relationship.

I love how Cat always looks out for others. Her huge heart is one of the many things I love about her.

Opening a second shop in Ann Arbor is on the horizon. Cat loves clothes, and a ton of people in Ann Arbor have the money to buy them. So it's a win-win.

"Everett," Cat's father comes up behind me and huffs out my name. "Come with me."

I look at Cat, and she shrugs, so I get up from the

table and follow him into a back room of the restaurant. It looks like a separate room for private parties.

"Now, I have something for you." He pulls a diamond ring out of his pocket and hands it to me. "It was Caterina's grandmother's ring—my mother." His English isn't as flawless as Cat's, but it's very good.

"Oh, okay," I say for lack of anything better.

"Now, we're going to do this right this time. You see, the first one"—there's an air of disgust in his voice—"did everything wrong. He stole our Caterina out from under us and treated her horribly. As a father, it makes me so…" His face turns red with anger.

"I know, sir. I'm sorry she had to go through that," I offer.

He nods slowly. "Yes, it was awful, but it helped her grow into the person and mother she is today. She's an incredible mother, no?"

"The best," I agree.

"I like you," he says. "I can tell you're good, unlike the other one. You're like my wife and me. How do they say, 'meant to be'? You make Caterina happy, and you love her the way you should. I can see that in your eyes, the way you look at her—so much love. So you must do right by her."

He looks at the diamond ring now in my hand. "When my mother was proposed to, it was tradition to gather both sides of the family for the engagement. Both the father of the bride and the groom would bow to each other seven times and shake hands to signify the blessing of the engagement. Now, that tradition has lost popularity over the years, and your family's not here, of course. But I would still like you to honor Caterina's family by proposing while everyone is gathered together. It's a sign of respect toward all who love her."

"Oh, you want me to propose tonight?" I attempt to hide the shock in my voice.

"You want to marry my daughter, do you not?" His wide eyes, the color of Cat's, hold me in a stare.

I hadn't planned on officially proposing this very second, but of course I want to marry Cat. "Yes, I love her very much."

"You'll love her and protect her always?" he asks.

"Yes, absolutely."

"Good. Then it's settled." He offers his hand, and I shake it.

"Should I go out and propose now?" I ask.

"I think now is as a good a time as any." He opens the door and motions me out.

Well, okay then…I guess we're doing this now.

We return to the main part of the restaurant, where Cat and her entire extended family eat and chat. It's loud and boisterous. Family members pass Benny around, admiring her adorable cheeks.

Cat notices when I return and gives me a look as if to ask if everything is okay. I simply nod.

My future father-in-law whistles, and everyone

turns our way. I press my lips together to stop from laughing as this is the weirdest situation ever. This whole night is going to be a comical antidote we tell our friends for years to come.

I approach Cat and take her hand in mine.

"What are you doing?" she asks under her breath.

I give her a reassuring smile.

"Cat." I clear my throat and speak loud enough for the entire restaurant full of family to hear. "I have had so much fun meeting your family tonight." I shoot a quick look toward her father, who nods proudly. "It's clear that you come from a long line of really great people. I know how important family is to you, so I wanted to say this while everyone is here."

"Seriously…what are you doing?" Cat whispers, her eyes wide.

I continue. "Our relationship hasn't been conventional by any means, but it's been amazing. My life truly started the day I met you because you—Caterina Avilova Araya—are everything to me. You are the most kind, beautiful, and incredible woman I've ever met. You're the best friend, daughter, partner, and mother there is. It's an honor to know you, but it's a gift to be loved by you."

I kneel on one knee before her and hold up her late grandmother's ring.

Cat gasps and covers her mouth with her hands.

"I don't know if I'll ever be worthy, but I hope you'll

let me show you just how much I love you for the rest of our lives. I promise to love and protect you with everything I am, always. Cat, my beautiful Cat, will you marry me?"

She kneels before me, our faces now level. "Are you serious?" she says in a quiet voice.

"As a heart attack." I wink.

"So we're going to get married?" she squeals.

"If you say yes." I grin.

"Oh my gosh. It's crazy, but everything else has been up to this point, hasn't it?"

I nod. "I'd say so."

"Yes! I will marry you, Everett West."

She throws her arms around my neck, and our mouths meet in a joyous kiss. The crowd of family members in the restaurant cheer and clap as I slide the ring onto her finger.

Cat peppers kisses all over my face before hugging me again. "I need to know what my father said to you." She giggles.

"Oh, I'll tell you all about it tonight." I chuckle.

"You're sure about this?" she questions once more.

"Absolutely. No doubt in my mind."

We partied late into the night, and I consumed more vodka than I have since my college fraternity days. Cat's family knows how to celebrate, that's for sure.

Her apartment is a short walk from the restaurant. It's elegantly styled and comfortable at the same time, which is exactly how I pictured it would be.

She lays Benny down in her crib and meets me in the kitchen, where I'm pounding water like it's my job.

"That was fun." She steps up behind me and slides the palms of her hands under my shirt, splaying them across my abdomen.

"A little too much." I chuckle, turning around to face her.

I tuck a strand of her hair behind her ear. "I love you so much."

"I love you, too." She smiles and leans her head against my chest. "So you had no intention of getting engaged when the night started?"

"Nope," I answer.

"But then my father had the talk with you?"

"Yep."

"And no regrets?"

I lean back and cup her face. "Are you kidding? Absolutely not. I didn't plan to propose tonight, but I always planned on proposing at some point. I didn't chase you halfway around the world to casually date." I laugh.

"Alright. Just checking. I just want to make sure you're in this a hundred percent. Because I am."

"My love, I am in this a hundred thousand, million percent," I say.

She puckers her lips. "I don't think that's a thing."

"Oh, it's a thing." I grin. "Now, I would like to make love to my future wife as long as she understands that I am not in prime form tonight. If there is anything I have learned about your father tonight, it's that he can hold his vodka way better than I can."

Cat laughs. "I'm pretty sure you were drunk that first marathon sex day at the casino hotel, and you did better than fine."

"Drunk or maybe a little tipsy, yes. But wasted…no."

She unbuttons my jeans. "I think you'll do just fine." She slides her hand into my pants.

The second she touches me, the blur of the night's vodka leaves my brain, and my focus is clear. She pulls my pants down to my ankles and drops to her knees, taking me into her mouth.

"Oh, shit…" I release a moan and steady myself against the countertop. My head falls back, and I relish the way Cat's mouth—my future wife's mouth—feels. Fucking perfection.

Leaning forward, I hook my hands under her arms and pull her up. "Have I told you lately how much I love you?" I cup her face and press my thumb against her wet lips.

"Yeah, I'm pretty sure this new accessory says it all." She holds her hand out, displaying her engagement ring.

Holding her hips, I rotate positions until her back is against the countertop. I remove her clothes until she's bare before me, and I lift her onto the granite.

I push her knees to the side and spread her legs. I position myself at her entrance. She releases a whimper in anticipation. "No one will ever love you as much as I do." I lean forward and pull her bottom lip into my mouth.

"I'm counting on it," she whispers against my lips with a sigh.

Grabbing my ass, she pulls me toward her. I groan as she takes every last inch of me inside her perfect body. I start to move, for all I want to do is make love to my girl until she screams my name.

Which she will.

…It will be heaven.

CHAPTER 30

CAT

*E*verett has officially been with me in Moscow for an entire month. It was longer than we planned to stay, but once the engagement happened, the wedding planning started, much to our surprise. I guess I thought Everett and I would have as long as we wanted to plan a wedding—something small and meaningful to take place back home in Michigan. Yet my parents had other plans.

They argued that my entire extended family couldn't afford to fly to the United States to witness my wedding. And since I had run away and eloped my first time around, it was only right that I give them this. They have a point. I did steal all the traditional parent of the bride responsibilities from them when I married Stephen.

He had wanted it to be just the two of us and pushed my desire to have my family present aside. Looking back, I should've known then. The fact that he didn't understand how important family was to me proved that he didn't know me very well.

Everett is the complete opposite of Stephen. He's game for everything that I, or my family, want. When he flew here to win me back, he had no idea that in four short weeks we'd be married. Yet he's handling it like a champ. The two of us spoke, and we're going to have a traditional Russian wedding for my family, and then when we go home to Ann Arbor, we're going to have a laid-back wedding for our Michigan family and friends. Because weddings here…are intense. They're a two-day affair, at minimum. Though, some celebrations can last up to a week.

The irony that this is all moving very quickly is not lost on me. I vowed the second time I would take it slow, but the truth is that once I dropped my walls and let Everett in, I was all in. I have no worries or reservations. He's it for me. Forever.

This past month has been incredible. Everett has worked virtually while I've been helping Anya transition from an employee to a manager in the shop. She's going to be amazing.

Everett, Benny, and I have been soaking up every minute as a family. It's been seamless as if it were always meant to be. And I believe it was. I can't imagine being with anyone else. Everett is the one person on this earth entirely compatible with me. We were destined to meet in that casino, there is no doubt in my mind.

I don't need a long engagement to make sure he's the one. He simply is.

Everything about him makes everything about me better. He loves unconditionally. He makes me laugh and sets my skin aflame with just a look. He loves our daughter and has worked hard to get to know my family.

I was hurt for so long. I felt deceived in my past relationship, but looking back and seeing what I have now, I don't regret a second of it. This was always meant to be my path. I met Everett at the exact moment I was supposed to.

Over the past decade, I've grown so much as a person. I've created bonds with incredible people I'd never have met had it not been for Stephen. I blossomed into this person who is a perfect partner for Everett and gave him time to grow up to be a perfect partner for me.

From the moment I married Stephen, Everett was always going to find me at that casino bar a decade later to pick up the pieces of my broken heart. Our fate was written in the stars, and because I truly believe that, I'm thrilled to be able to marry him today. Because this too, was meant to be.

"Oh, mi hija," my mother exclaims as she enters the dressing room of the church. She cradles my face in her hands. "Preciosa. Perfección."

"No one is perfect, Mamá."

"You are, mi amor. Always have been."

Her gaze travels over my dress, and she smiles wide with tears in her eyes. She raises her hands. "Perfección," she says again.

My mermaid-style gown is sleeveless and made from white silk that hugs my body until it opens up to a long train behind me. It's simple and elegant. The veil is a masterpiece as it extends all the way down my back and to the ground.

I feel like a princess, and I couldn't be happier.

The ceremony is being held in an old orthodox church, per tradition. My mother made sure I would be married in one of the most beautiful places in Moscow. It literally looks like a castle from a princess story. It's situated on the Pakhra River and surrounded by pristinely kept greenery. Inside, the walls are filled with ornate baby blue and ivory sculptures. As one walks down the aisle, it feels like heaven. Simply stunning.

My entire family, both Russian, and Spanish, are here to celebrate with Everett and me. It's overwhelming. I feel so lucky that it doesn't feel quite real. Maybe that's how true love is meant to feel—unreal.

My mother kisses both of my cheeks. "Your dad is just outside the room. I'll see you in there." She beams up at me, pride in her expression.

I follow her out to meet my father in the grand atrium. He too has tears in his eyes when he sees me, and I'm so happy we decided to get married here where my family could be a part of it. Looking at it through a parents' perspective, I realize now how much my first marriage must've hurt them. I'd be heartbroken if Benny ran off and got married without me someday.

"You are so beautiful, my love," my father says as I take his arm.

"Thank you, Dad."

The organ begins playing, indicating that it's time to walk down the aisle. I hold my bouquet of daisies in my grasp. It was a simple choice for such an extravagant day. My mom questioned the flowers a few times, but it had to be this way. The daisies are simple, beautiful, and happy…just like my relationship with Everett. In this grandiose place for this extravagant event where everything is over the top, they are a grounding symbol of how our life will be. For I don't need all the glitz and glamour, I just need Everett and our family. It's not the things that make life worth living. It's the people.

I will always be his *Daisy*, and he will always be the love of my life.

Tears fall from his eyes as I walk down the aisle. His

stare radiates pure love and devotion, and I've never felt luckier.

My mother sits in the front row with Bernadette on her lap. Our baby looks adorable in her poufy white dress as she flaps her arms in excitement.

My father blesses the marriage and leaves us with the priest for the ceremony. The entire event is a blur. I go through the motions, but all I think about is Everett and how, in a few short moments, I will officially be his wife, and he, my husband.

"I love you," he mouths as the priest speaks to the congregation.

"I love you." I smile wide.

Everett and I are crowned by the priest, as per tradition. After the crowns are placed atop our heads, we are given a glass of wine by the priest to signify our journey into married life.

When we are finally announced man and wife, we're each given a crystal glass by my parents.

"What do I do with this?" Everett asks.

"You must break it into as many pieces as possible. Each shard supposedly signifies one year of happy marriage." I tell him.

"Oh, okay." He raises the glass in the air. "Then you better smash it good because there will be many happy years," he says.

"Deal." I nod.

We throw our glasses against the tiled floor, and the glasses shatter into more pieces than years we have left in life. So I feel confident that we're going to be happy until the very end.

* * *

Russian weddings can last up to a week. My family celebrated for three full days. I've danced more than I have in my entire life. My face hurts from smiling, and the thought of another sip of anything but water makes my stomach sour. The most shocking of all, I couldn't be paid to put on a pair of heels anytime soon.

"Just throw them out." I glare at my closet full of shoes. "They are not coming back to America with us."

My husband sits at the end of the sofa with my foot between his hands. He massages the ball of my foot, careful to avoid the massive blisters on my toes and the back of my heel.

"You don't mean that. You're just going through a rough patch," he teases.

I shake my head. "No, I mean it. I'm done with uncomfortable footwear. You know I thought my feet were immune to torture at this point. Leave it to an Avilova wedding to kill my feet for good." I groan as my head falls back onto the sofa pillows when Everett pushes his thumb against the arch of my foot.

"Well, whatever you decide, I support you," he says.

I lift my head and, in all seriousness, say, "I'm going to be a Croc person now."

Everett presses his lips in a line to suppress a smile.

"What? I am. Crocs? Or maybe flip-flops? Heck… slippers. They are my new footwear choice. You want to go on a date? I'm wearing slippers."

Everett clears his throat and raises a brow. "You know, slippers might not have been an awful choice for the reception. Could've avoided a lot of pain."

"Yes." I wave my hand through the air, my mother's Spanish accent coming through as it often does when I'm angry. "Hindsight is twenty-twenty, as they say."

"Oh, you're getting spicy. I've never really seen you so fiery. Three days into marriage, and your true colors are shining through." He grins, setting my foot down on the sofa. "I'm not going to lie. It's a turn-on." He comes over to my side of the couch and lays beside me, kissing my temple.

I playfully push him away. "You're crazy."

"Crazy for you, my love."

"We have to pack up this place…and my feet hurt," I whine.

He wraps his arm around my middle and snuggles into my side. "I will take care of it. You, just direct."

I press my lips to his. "I love you."

"Can you do me a favor, though?" he asks.

"Of course."

"Tell your father we're out sightseeing or something…anything to keep him away. Last night, he mentioned something about more celebrating. I'm telling you right now…if he shows up with a bottle of vodka…I can't. In fact, I'm pretty sure that particular drink is ruined for life."

I giggle. "Yeah, we don't take celebrations lightly."

"That much is clear."

"I'll tell him we have plans today. Okay?"

"Thank you." He plants another kiss on my lips.

I thread my fingers through his hair and pull his face closer, deepening our kiss.

After a moment, I pull back. "Hey, if I would've puked at some point during our three-day reception, would you feel different about me?"

He laughs. "No, I would've puked along with you… which honestly, I'd probably feel better if I had. Would you feel different about me if my breath was bad and my tongue was white with bacteria?"

I quirk a brow. "Honestly, your breath could've knocked out a family of five this morning. But I don't love you any less." I pucker my lips for a kiss.

He smacks his lips against mine. "This really is true love."

"I'd say so." My grin falls when the sound of Benny crying from the other room reaches us.

"I got her." Everett smiles before jumping off the sofa with more pep than someone who's been drunk for seventy-two hours should have.

As Everett walks away to retrieve our daughter, my chest fills with gratitude. In this whirlwind of events—with our speedy courtship, engagement, and marriage—I've grown to love this man I now call my husband, more every second. And I don't see that ever changing.

CHAPTER 31

EVERETT

"Oh, my goodness, she is a superstar!" I chant, clapping my hands as Benny crawls toward me with an adorable giggle. "Go! Go! Go!"

She giggles louder, spit bubbles flying out of her mouth as she crawls.

When she reaches me, I scoop her up in my arms. Lifting her dress, I blow raspberries on her belly and am rewarded with another round of giggles.

"How did you get so talented? Your daddy? You got your super speed from your daddy, didn't you?"

At six months and a couple weeks old, Benny is meeting all her baby milestones and actually exceeding many of them. We found her a pediatrician in Ann

Arbor, and when the doctor checked off the six-month milestones at her appointment last week, I couldn't have been more proud.

Cat laughed at me, stating that all babies develop differently, and even if she wasn't reaching her milestones, it would be fine. *She'll do things in her own time*, she said. To which, I reply, "Heck yeah, ahead of schedule because she's freaking brilliant."

"You know, Daddy was super fast, too. I went to the state track meet in high school and won first place in the 4 x 100 relay. I'm pretty sure my split still holds the record at my old high school. I should actually check on that," I tell my daughter. "Being fast is in your genes."

Laughter comes from across the room. "Would you stop?" Cat shakes her head. "She can't even walk yet. We have no idea if she's going to be a track star."

"She is." I shoot my wife a mock glare and speak to Benny again. "Momma may be skeptical, but she needs to realize that speed is in your genes."

Cat grabs some lip gloss from the table and puts it on. "You know, she may not even like running…or sports. Maybe she'll go to States for chess or violin."

I playfully cover Benny's ears and gasp in mock disgust. "Watch your mouth," I joke. "Plus, I don't know if chess players compete at a state level."

"Well, whatever she decides to do, she'll be perfect as long as she's happy," Cat says.

I bounce Benny up and down. "Well, obviously

because she's already absolutely perfect," I say in a very unmanly baby voice.

"You ready? People are going to be getting here soon." Cat looks toward the mirror and breaks up one of her long curls. She's absolutely stunning.

She's wearing a simple satin A-line wedding dress with a flowy skirt. I know what an A-line dress is now thanks to my fashionista wife. Her feet have healed, and she's made up with her killer heels. She looks like a woman straight out of a fashion magazine.

We moved back to Ann Arbor a few weeks ago without telling anyone. We knew we wanted to celebrate our wedding with our friends and family here. When talking about how to do it, Cat decided she wanted to make it a surprise. She said she'd always wanted to throw a surprise birthday party so we're throwing a surprise wedding.

The past few weeks have been intense. We bought a house, a beautiful home, only a block away from Cat's best friend, Alma. It's in a picturesque neighborhood and has a large tree-lined backyard. It's as much privacy as anyone living in a neighborhood could hope for.

No one from Michigan knows anything. We've kept our arrival and marriage a secret…well, until today. We knew it'd be important for the people we love to celebrate with us. So a simple little surprise backyard wedding is the way we're doing it.

Good food, fun, and love…on a beautiful day.

Our wedding planner, Felicity, scurries into the room. "Guests are arriving. I have them waiting in the front room. They have no idea what's going on. I will start seating them in a bit." She claps her hands together and looks around the room like she's forgetting something. "I have never done a surprise wedding, and this is seriously the best. It looks like a fairy garden outside… and the weather?" She kisses her fingers. "Chef's kiss." "You never know. Late September can be the most beautiful weather or the worst. You know you lucked out."

Our wedding planner came highly recommended and for good a reason. She's great at what she does. She transformed our backyard into something straight from a movie. But the girl likes to talk—a lot. I can't say I'm going to miss her when today is done.

She scans Cat and turns to Benny and me. I'm wearing a light gray suit, and Benny is in a poufy mini-wedding dress, as I like to call it.

"You are all magazine worthy." She kisses her fingers again. "Chef's kiss," she says again. She says that a lot—a little too much—but this time, I can't disagree. We are a great-looking family.

"You have the list?" Cat says. "Make sure those people are all here before you call us down. Especially Everett's mom, Sarah."

"Yes, she is perpetually late, but it's important that she's here," I chime in.

"Well, her invitation clearly said to be on time," Felicity notes.

"That doesn't mean she will be." I shrug.

"Okay, I will start seating people, and when your mother arrives, we'll begin. The orchestra is ready. I have my assistant in place to release the butterflies. So the three of you will walk down together, and then I have Benny's frilly princess carriage at the end of the aisle. There are toys in there to hopefully keep her occupied while you two say your vows," Felicity yammers.

"If not, we'll just pick her up. She can be part of the vows," I say.

"Right. Well, let's just hope it doesn't come to that," Felicity says in all seriousness, and I have to stop myself from laughing. "You have your bouquet?" she asks Cat.

"I sure do."

"Okay, I'll be back when it's time." Felicity nods and turns on her heel, scurrying out of the room.

"Butterflies?" I raise a brow. "When did that happen? And what has become of our simple backyard wedding?" I laugh.

"I know." Cat raises her arms, palms up. "Felicity."

I nod in understanding. "That's all you have to say."

Cat grins. "It does look amazing out there, though. It's going to be so much fun."

"What do you think everyone's thinking?" I ask.

"I mean, once they're seated, they'll know it's a

wedding. How could they not? But they'll have no idea that it's a second wedding or that this is our house."

"True. I can't wait to eat. I'm starving." I rub my stomach for dramatic effect. The reception is being catered by a few of the best restaurants in Ann Arbor. We couldn't agree on a menu, so we're going with Mexican, barbecue, and Mediterranean. It's random… but delicious.

"Felicity made you the kale energy shake. Didn't you drink yours?" Cat questions.

"No, I didn't, babe. First, it was green with random purple lumps."

"Those were chia seeds. They give you energy." Cat sits down on the loveseat before standing back up, afraid to wrinkle her dress.

"Regardless, I think it's a little bit out of the realm of responsibility of a wedding planner to have her prepare our meals and tell us what to eat. We hired her to put on a wedding, not make us smoothies."

"She only wants to make sure everything run smoothly today, and that includes eating well." Cat shrugs.

I chuckle. "Come on. It's too much."

She grins, looking down. "It's a little much. Still…you should've drunk it. You wouldn't be hungry right now if you had."

"I highly doubt that." I scoff.

I leave Benny to roll around on the ground. She lies

on her back and holds her foot to her mouth. Her latest obsession with toes will keep her busy for a while.

I walk up behind Cat and pull her soft waves to the side and kiss her bare shoulder. "Have I told you lately how incredibly lucky I am to be marrying you today…again?"

She grins. "A few times." Reaching back, she cradles the side of my face in her hand. "I'm just so excited to have everything we've been doing out in the open and get to celebrate with our friends."

"Yeah, it's going to be an epic party. When are the fairies going to arrive with their magic dust allowing us all to fly?" I wrap my arms around her waist and pull her back against my front.

"I'm not sure, but if there is such a thing as fairies, Felicity will get them here."

"Are you going to miss her?"

She turns to face me and circles her arms around my neck. "Yes and no. I know it sounds silly because, well, we're already married, but I've had so much fun planning this surprise wedding. I realize we agreed to a simple backyard celebration, but the more that Felicity and I talked over the options, the more I wanted. I'm just so happy, and I want the magic of the day to express that. This is our last wedding." She gives me a sheepish look because normally couples only get one to begin with. "And I want it to be perfect. Don't get me wrong, our first wedding was wonderful, too. But it wasn't us. It was for my parents and my family. I want this one to symbolize everything we are."

I furrow my brow with a playful pucker of my lips. "Are you saying that the butterflies weren't completely Felicity's idea?"

"I cannot confirm or deny…"

I plant a kiss on her lips. "It's fine, babe. Whatever makes you happy. If you're happy, I am, too."

"I'm kind of bummed that we aren't going to be celebrating for three whole days." She frowns.

I laugh. "I can guarantee your feet and my liver completely disagree."

"It's been such a magical few months. I don't want it to end. I want to always feel this way with you."

The corners of my mouth tilt up. Lifting my arm, I push a lock of hair off her face. "Every day together will be incredible. Our life is going to be one big adventure. A wedding is just the start. We have so much to look forward to. We have all of Benny's milestones and birthday parties. We'll have family outings exploring new places. We'll have more kids, and you'll get to experience it with me by your side. We'll have holidays and anniversaries…and every Monday, Tuesday, Wednesday, Thursday, Friday, Saturday… and Sunday because every day spent together is going to be amazing because we're together. I don't care if we're swimming under a waterfall in Costa Rica or washing the dishes after dinner—I'm looking forward to every second."

She smiles with trembling lips as tears come to her eyes. "That sounds good."

"I've told you before, but I'll tell you again. You are everything I've ever wanted in a partner, Cat. I will cherish every moment in this life together and make sure that you always know how much you're loved."

She nods and kisses me. "Thank you, my love."

"You feel better?"

"Absolutely." She kisses me again.

"Good. That was a pretty kick-ass speech. I should just repeat that for my vows." I lower my hands from her waist and squeeze her ass.

She yelps and smacks me on the chest. "You better have written something, mister. You had three weeks."

I kiss her forehead and step back. "I'll wing it."

"Everett!" she chastises, causing me to laugh.

"I'm kidding. Of course, I wrote my vows."

"Appropriate vows?" She lifts a brow.

"Well, I can't promise that." I shoot her a wink.

CHAPTER 32

CAT

Every girl dreams of a fairy-tale life, and while that fairy tale varies between each girl, the fact that there is a dream is the same. I wanted an incredible love, a man who would go to the ends of the earth for me, a prince who would fight kingdoms and slay dragons if that's what it took to be with me.

Not everyone finds their prince, but I found mine. The timeline wasn't what I thought it'd be, but in the end, all that matters is I reached my destination, and now I get to enjoy my happily ever after for the rest of my life.

Not a sliver of my former battered, skeptic heart is

left to doubt anything involving Everett. His love has made my heart whole. The worry and fear have dissipated. Piece by piece. Each kiss, loving look, kind word, and thoughtful touch from Everett has given me the power to fully live the life I'm meant to have.

I'm so happy that it almost doesn't feel real, but I never doubt for a second that it is.

Everett holds our perfect little princess in one arm while the hand from his other grasps mine.

"You ready, Mrs. West?" He squeezes my hand.

"Definitely." I hold my bouquet at my waist with my other hand.

The violins begin the breathtaking melody, and my family starts our journey down the grassy path lined with flower petals. The joyous and surprised faces of our friends and family are incredible. There are cheers and gasps, smiles and tears. Every single person looks utterly thrilled for us, and I know they are. Everett and I have surrounded ourselves with some pretty great people.

Felicity, in all her over-the-top ways, came through. She transformed this space into something truly magical. The flowers, twinkle lights, greenery, music, and moss-covered trees surround us in a real-life dream come true. I feel like a queen walking through my garden with my king.

I'm so glad we did this wedding because this is

exactly how our journey to love has felt—magical, and now our friends get to experience it with us. This will always be one of the best days of my life.

* * *

"Oh, my gosh. You have to try this stuffed mushroom, babe." Everett shoves a mushroom toward my mouth, and I laugh as I bite it.

The only wedding details he insisted on being a part of was the food. So I'm glad the giant spread of dishes has met his expectations. Felicity made a good call when she ordered fancy to-go containers. Everyone here is going to be able to take home enough food to feed them for a week. Like everything else pertaining to today, we might have gone a tad overboard.

"So?" He waits for my response.

I give him a thumbs-up and cover my mouth with my hand before speaking. "So good," I say through a mouth full of mushroom and cream cheese.

"Right? I knew you would love those." He leans in and kisses me.

The party is in full swing. The string quartet has been replaced with a live band, and the dance floor is getting lots of use. I nursed Benny, and Sarah, Everett's mom, insisted on rocking her to sleep. I told her that Benny would simply lie down and go to sleep, but I could tell she wanted to rock her. I get it. My mom was the same way, getting in as much snuggles with the baby as she could.

Sarah hasn't stopped smiling all night, and I'm so grateful that she gets to see her son truly happy. I know that's always been a worry for her. Benny really warmed up to her, as well. I can tell we're going to have loads of grandma time ahead of us, and I can't wait. There's nothing better than family.

Everett has briefly left the food table to dance with some of his college friends. I recognize Asher, Cassie, Tannon, and her husband, Jude. There are others that I don't know. I'm assuming they're fraternity brothers from college. There is still so much to learn about my husband, and it's exciting.

Quinn and Alma come over to me after stopping at the bar.

"I can't believe you threw together this wedding in three weeks." Quinn shakes her head. "I mean, I went all out for mine, and it took me a year to plan...and still, it was nothing like this."

"Hey, yours had a bouncy house and a water slide," Alma reminds her. "That's not nothing."

"Yeah, the two things my husband planned." She chuckles.

"But, seriously, Cat. It felt like we were in a fairy wonderland. I'm not kidding. At the end, when all the butterflies were released...for a moment, I thought it was Tinker Bell and her friends." Quinn nods, taking a sip of her wine.

"You did not." I laugh.

"No, for a moment…I almost believed."

"It was pretty magical." Alma grins.

I shrug. "Yeah, it was."

Quinn reaches out and squeezes my arm. "Well, I'm not surprised. Everything you do is perfect. So of course today was but…the fact that no one knew what they were walking into, the whole surprise factor…that threw me for a loop."

Alma nods. "Yeah, that was great. Not what I'd expect from you but so cool."

"You're right. I'm such a planner, but the past year has proved that the best things in life aren't planned. I thought it went with the theme of our love story," I say.

"Oh, definitely," Alma and Quinn say in unison.

"And Everett's such a good guy. I've really gotten to know him over the past couple of years, and he's truly one of the good ones. It doesn't hurt that he's gorgeous, too," Quinn adds.

I smile wide. "Yeah. He is the best and very hot. No doubt about that."

"I know it's not the time tonight, but let's get together this week to look at pictures and videos from your other wedding. The bits and pieces I've heard make it sound incredible, too," Alma suggests.

"It was incredible. Different but wonderful. We

incorporated many traditions to make my father and his family happy, and I'm glad we did. I'll never forget it. But today was for us, you know?"

Quinn nods. "Yeah, I totally get that. What was your favorite part about that wedding?"

"Well, besides the obvious, marrying Everett…it was the dress. Gorgeous. A little too formal for this wedding but still, I'll have to show you. I have it upstairs."

"Oh, my gosh. Yes, please," Quinn says. "We need to get together soon for a housewarming party. Obviously, the new house isn't the focus tonight, but it's awesome."

"I know. We lucked out finding it," I say.

"And I love that it's so close to us." Alma grins.

"Me, too." I agree as its proximity to Alma was a huge draw to the house.

Alma wraps her arm around my waist and leans her head against my shoulder. "I'm so happy for you. You're one of the greatest people in the world, and you deserve this. I always wanted you to find your person. I can't remember ever seeing you happier."

Quinn smiles in agreement.

Alma's words bring tears to my eyes. "Thank you. It's true. I'm happier than I've ever been."

"Speaking of." Quinn motions toward the dance floor where Everett is waving me over.

"Oh, no." I sigh. "I swear my feet just healed from my first wedding's dancing shenanigans."

"Take 'em off," Alma says. "Go barefoot."

"Maybe in a bit. I mean, you must admit, these will look amazing in the pictures." I scrunch up my nose and kick out my leg, displaying my white satin heels.

"OMG. Yes. They're perfection," Quinn says in dramatic fashion. I can always count on her to understand my style.

"Come on. Let's dance." I wave for them to follow.

When I reach Everett, he pulls me into an embrace. "I missed you." His mouth captures mine.

"I missed you," I echo.

He takes hold of my hips as I move them to the upbeat music. After a couple minutes of dancing, he says, "I got you a present," and extends his hand. I take it, and he leads us off the dance floor.

He hands me a box wrapped with silver paper and a white ribbon. I smile big and quickly pull off the paper to reveal a pair of white Crocs. I throw my head back in laughter. "You know I'm not wearing these! I may have mentioned them during a moment of darkness and despair, and while I appreciate the thought, I wouldn't be caught dead in these."

He laughs with me. "I know. That's why I got you these." He hands me another box wrapped in the same silver paper.

I open it to reveal adorable satin ballet slippers. "Oh, my gosh." I hold my hand to my chest.

"For my princess."

"Everett, I love them. They match my dress."

"And they're comfortable. Tonight should be perfect…which means no blisters."

"Okay." I nod.

"Okay? As in you'll wear them?" he questions.

"I'll wear them." I take a seat in a chair and extend my feet.

Everett drops to one knee and undoes the straps of my high-heeled shoes and pulls them off. One by one, he slides my feet into the ballet slippers.

"A perfect fit." I wiggle my toes.

"For my queen." He stands and takes my hand, pulling me up with him. "Let's dance."

He leads me back out onto the dance floor, where the band is now playing a slow song. I circle my arms around his neck, and he takes hold of my waist, pulling me close. I feel his heartbeat against mine and melt into him. I sway to the music with my husband, and it's another perfect moment.

As I dance with my husband, memories from our journey play through my mind. I still can't believe it all played out the way it did. One small variation in our timeline could've changed everything.

"Thank you for finding me twice and never giving up on us." I pull in a grateful breath.

"You were always destined to be mine, my Daisy. I would've found you a thousand times if I had to."

His words resonate deep within my soul, and I know he's right. No matter how the petals of fate fall, the last one will always land on one singular truth…

…he loves me.

EPILOGUE

EVERETT

The thing about true destiny is that there's no denying it, no arguing about it, and no avoiding it. It's going to happen. That's the entire meaning of the word. Very few things in life are actually destined. Coincidental? Sure. Desired? Absolutely. Destined. No.

Destiny is reserved for the most special parts of life, the truest gifts.

My daughter.

My son.

My wife.

My entire purpose on this earth is to love them, and I'm eternally grateful for it.

Our son, Hayes, arrived a month shy of Benny's second birthday, and Cat's parents and grandmother moved to Michigan in time to attend Bernadette's second birthday party.

In fact, they live in the house to the right of ours.

As fate would have it, our next-door neighbors put their house up for sale during Cat's pregnancy with Hayes. When her parents found out, they retired, sold everything, and moved in next door. They say that Cat grew up and left so young, and they didn't want to miss anything with their grandbabies. I don't blame them.

Although I had my reservations when the idea was first presented to me, having my in-laws so close has been incredible. They're respectful of our space and privacy, yet they're always there for the kids and us.

Cat and I go out at least once every couple of weeks, and her parents love to babysit. My wife looks forward to our date nights. I always try to make them unique and special. She says it reminds her of our whirlwind two-week speed dating adventure. She loves reminiscing about those fourteen days. I'd never tell her and risk tarnishing her fond memories, but I hated the way I felt during that time. In one word, I felt desperate. I was terrified of losing her because I knew I'd never get over it if I did. Luckily, I don't have to worry about that because there's nothing I trust in more than us.

I started my own internet consulting firm, and it's really taken off. I get to work from home when it's convenient for my family while providing an incredible life. Cat opened a boutique in downtown Ann Arbor shortly after our wedding and loves it.

After an exorbitant amount of persuasion, I finally convinced my mother to move into a townhouse that we purchased for her nearby. There are a lot of things I wish were different from my childhood, but the one aspect I never questioned is my mother's love for me. I know she took care of me the very best she could, and now I want to take care of her.

She loves being closer to her grandkids and gets along great with Cat's parents. She's too proud to admit it, but I know she's glad to be out of her old apartment and neighborhood.

So now, we're surrounded by friends and family—a perfect community in which to raise our greatest two blessings.

"Dad, I'm ready," my nine-year-old daughter calls from the rubber "home base" set up in our backyard baseball diamond.

Benny is the spitting image of her mother. She's absolutely beautiful with the spirit of a warrior. She loves sports and wants to play them all. She not only wants to play them, but she wants to be "better than the boys." She's fiercely competitive, and I love it.

"Right. Gotcha." I turn to Hayes, who kicks at the grass next to first base. "Get ready, bud."

He nods, excited though the dandelion in the grass

will pull his attention from the game at any moment. At seven, Hayes still plays T-ball, where he hits the ball off a tee instead of having a coach pitch. He could try out for coach pitch, but to be fair, he's not that into it. I think he continues to play because his older sister does, but he'd rather be building his Lego creations at home. Maybe he'll like sports when he's older, or maybe he won't. It doesn't bother me either way as long as he's happy.

I pitch the ball over home plate, and Benny hits it hard. It goes flying over my head.

"Hayes, the ball, man," I call out.

Hayes looks from me to his sister, who is racing toward him, and then to the grass a distance behind second base where the ball has landed. "Oh, yeah!" He grins and sprints toward the ball.

Benny sprints around second base, and I run toward home, ready to catch the ball after Hayes retrieves it.

"Throw it hard," I tell him as Benny bolts toward me.

My daughter pounds her foot against home base, and a couple of seconds later, I catch the ball with my mitt.

"Good throw, Hayes!" I smile and then turn to Benny, who's hugging Cat as the girls' team celebrates their home run. "Great job, Ben."

"Thanks, Dad." She beams.

"The girls are winning," Cat teases as she and Benny do a silly victory dance.

"We're not keeping score." I narrow my eyes. "This is just for fun, right?"

"Um, Dad. Only losers don't keep score." Benny gives her mom a high five.

I shake my head and laugh.

My mother-in-law steps outside onto our deck. "Dinner's ready!" she calls.

Another perk to having a former restaurant owner who loves to cook living next door is the food. We never go hungry in the West household, that's for sure.

"Yes!" Hayes cheers and drops his baseball glove. "Abuela made chocolate cake for dessert, too!"

"Oh, I can't wait." Benny runs after her brother. One thing the two of them can always agree on is food. Like me, they love to eat—sweets, especially.

I extend my hand toward Cat, and she entwines her fingers through mine as we leisurely walk toward the house.

She leans her head against my shoulder with a content sigh.

I kiss the top of her head. "I love you."

"I love you." She squeezes my hand.

My chest aches with love—for this woman, for our family, and for this life. I don't know what I did to deserve such happiness, but I'm not questioning it. Not a second goes by when I'm not grateful. Not everyone gets the happily ever after, but I'm so fortunate that I did.

* * *

CAT

"Oh, my gosh! What are we doing?" I chuckle as my husband parks in the large aquarium's abandoned parking lot.

"You'll see." He grins. Shutting off the car, he gets out and walks around to open my door. I take his hand as I step out.

"We're not breaking and entering, are we?"

His face lights up. "That would be exciting. Wouldn't it?"

He leads me to the front doors of the aquarium, and my heart pumps rapidly within my chest. Logically, I know that Everett would never break into a building, especially with me in tow. Yet he has this way of keeping me on the edge of my seat.

Life with him is never boring.

Pulling a key out of his pocket, he unlocks the large entry door.

Once inside, he inputs a code into the security box on the wall.

The interior of the building is familiar as we've taken our kids to this aquarium a few times. The exhibits are lit up, showcasing all of the colorful fish, while the overhead lights are dimmed, creating a mysterious and romantic vibe.

"We have the whole place to ourselves? How did you do this?" I lean in toward Everett as we move farther into the building.

"I have my ways." He kisses my lips, soft and sweet.

I've always loved aquariums. The colorful fish swim around in the ocean-blue water as if they don't have a care in the world. It's serene—the whole experience brings me a sense of calm. Yet experiencing it without a large crowd of people takes it to a whole other level.

We stop at each tank and watch the sea creatures. It's so fun. I can't help but wish the kids were here. They would love this. When this night is over, I'll ask Everett if there's any way he can pull some strings again so that our children can see what I'm seeing.

Everett plans the best dates. He always has. He makes me feel like the luckiest woman in the world every second of every day. He loves fiercely—it's one of my favorite things about him. Early on in our marriage, we both agreed that we'd always make time for ourselves, and we have. It's important for children to be raised by parents who love each other. I hope we're setting an example for our kids of the kind of love they should seek—the real kind. Because true love is beautiful. It's kindness, respect, patience, and a deep level of adoration. It's loving a person to their core, faults and all.

Everett showed me what it felt like to be truly loved.

He is my one and only, and I'm thankful every day he found me.

We visit the stingray encounter. I reach my hand into the water and glide my fingertips across their smooth, rubbery skin. I love stingrays. They remind me of graceful birds of the ocean, flapping through the water. They're just happy. When I see them from beneath, they always look like they're grinning. Sure, maybe it's just the way their features appear, but I like to think they are smiling.

I giggle when one flaps its "wings" and splashes us with water. I turn to Everett to find him watching me with a huge smile on his face.

"Best date ever." I circle my arms around his neck and press my lips to his.

"You say that every time," he says.

"Because it's true."

He squeezes my butt and gives me a chaste kiss before saying, "Come on. I want to show you the best part."

"This isn't the best part?"

"You'll see."

He leads me toward the walking tunnel that goes through a giant fish tank. It's always been the best part of the aquarium because it feels like you're walking through the ocean, with sea life swimming by the glass on either side and above you.

Only this time, the stone edges to each side where people normally sit or children stand to watch the fish are lined with votive candles. I gasp, bringing my hands to my mouth, as the rows of flickering light line a floor filled with plush blankets and pillows. The blue glow from the aquarium dance across the ground, making it appear as if the linens are, in fact, placed at the bottom of the ocean floor.

A bottle of chilled wine in a silver bucket filled with ice and a wicker basket filled with packaged food—no doubt from one of my favorite restaurants.

I shake my head and drop my hands from my face. "No, this is definitely the best date ever."

"Come on." Everett grins and leads me toward the cushioned floor.

I take a seat and lean against some pillows as Everett pours me a glass of wine.

"For my beautiful wife." He hands me the wineglass.

"I have to know how you did this." I smile. "This is amazing, E."

He takes a sip of wine. "Well, the owner is a big client of mine."

"Well, I figured, but that still doesn't explain why he'd let you have this much access."

Everett shrugs. "What can I say? I'm a charming guy."

I laugh. "That's true."

My husband has always been someone who others gravitate toward. People just like him. He's witty and funny. He's charming and loyal. He comes off as trustworthy, and he is.

"So I thought we'd do a little throwback to the picnic

in the park that first week. I brought our favorite Mediterranean. Remember that date?" He grins.

"Of course I do. What I remember most is how much I wanted you to kiss me."

He nods. "Yeah, I recall how much I wanted you to give me permission to kiss you."

"Yeah, I was set in my ways."

"Still are," he adds.

"Hey." I hit him playfully on the chest.

He laughs and sets out glasses of wine on the ledge. "I'm not saying that's a bad thing. I love your ways. Your ways are the best." He scoots closer to me and wraps his arms around my waist.

"Yeah?"

"Yeah," he agrees before placing his lips against my neck.

He pulls my strappy silk top over my head and continues to kiss my skin—peppering soft kisses across my collarbone and up my neck.

I release a sigh of pleasure. "Babe. What about cameras?"

He unhooks the clasp of my bra, and it falls leaving me fully exposed. "I designed the security system here. All the cameras in this area have been turned off."

"Are you sure?"

"I'm positive." He takes my nipple in his mouth, and my head falls back in a groan. My entire body hums with need. "No one is going to see this body but me."

We make quick work of removing the remainder of our clothes. I lie back as Everett worships every inch of my body with his mouth.

"I love you." I pant as I come down from my release.

He kisses up my torso until his face hovers above mine. "I love you, Cat. More than I could ever show you."

I take his face between my palms and pull it to mine. Our tongues move with one another in the familiar dance that will never get old.

His hard length is at my entrance, teasing me. "Babe," I start to say until something else catches my attention. "A sea turtle is watching us."

Everett chuckles. "Ignore him. He's just jealous."

I stare at the turtle swimming overhead. "He's like seriously staring."

"Close your eyes," Everett orders in a husky whisper, and I do as instructed. "It's just you and me, always and forever."

As my husband enters me, everything fades away but our connection. It's just him and me in our own little world of bliss.

My forever favorite place to be.

THANK you so much for reading! I hope you loved Destined Souls!

Cassie and Asher's story, Entwined Souls, will be out

in December, and is the last story in the series. I love it so much!

Find Entwined Souls here.

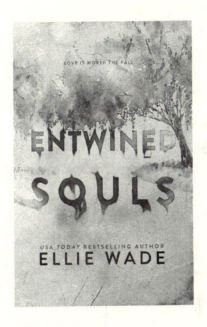

If you're new to this world, make sure to catch up on the other stories in The Beautiful Souls collection, starting with Bared Souls.

Dear Readers,

Oh, my goodness, Cat's story is out into the world! I'm so excited. As soon as Bared Souls was written, I knew that Cat would need her story told. Her journey took a while to come to me, but I'm thrilled with the result. I've always wanted to write a *one-night stand between strangers, oops baby love story.* Haha. It was perfect for Cat who'd always been so proper and tried to do everything "right." I love the internal struggle within Cat as she tried to figure out her path. I adore Everett and love the dynamic he brings to this world.

I hope you all loved it, too!

If you're reading this and have followed these characters' journeys…thank you! I love this world, and the people in it so much. To be honest, I'm still blown away with the response I've received from Bared Souls. I'm so grateful that readers have wanted to read beyond Alma and Leo and explore the lives of the rest of the characters.

The next, and probably last, book in the series is Cassie and Asher's story. I think their backstories and journey are so interesting and I can't wait to write about them. So stay tuned!

Thanks again for reading!

I truly appreciate all the support. Writing has always been my dream, and I couldn't do this without you.

DEAR READERS

Make your journey a beautiful one!

Love,

Ellie

ACKNOWLEDGMENTS

To my girls, the ones I message if I have a question, the ones that support me unconditionally, the ones that love me—I'm so grateful for all of you! Gala, Suzanne, Christine, Elle, Karrie, Amy C., Kylie, Amy E., and Kim—You all are so awesome. Seriously, each of you is a gift, and you have helped me in invaluable, different ways. I love you all so much. XOXO

To my cover artist, Letitia Hasser from RBA Designs—Thank you! Your work inspires me. You are a true artist, and I am so grateful to work with you. People do judge a book by its cover, so thank you for making mine *gorgeous*! XO

To my editors, Jenny Sims from Editing4Indies, and Kylie Ryan from Final Cut Editing—I love you both so much! Thank you for always fitting me in, and everything you do to make my words shine!

Lastly, to my loyal readers—I love you! Thank you for reaching out, reviewing, and sharing your book recs with your friends. There are seriously great people in this book community, and I am humbled by your support. Your messages breathe life into my writing and keep me going on this journey. Truly, thank you! Because of you, indie authors get their stories out. Thank you for supporting all authors and the great stories they write.

Readers—You can connect with me on several places, and I would love to hear from you.

Join my readers group: www.facebook.com/groups/wadeswarriorsforthehea

Find me on Facebook: www.facebook.com/EllieWadeAuthor

Find me on Instagram: www.instagram.com/authorelliewade

Find me on TikTok: https://www.tiktok.com/@authorelliewade

Visit my website: www.elliewade.com

Remember, the greatest gift you can give an author is a review. If you feel so inclined, please leave a review on the various retailer sites. It doesn't have to be fancy. A couple of sentences would be awesome!

I could honestly write a whole book about everyone in this world whom I am thankful for. I am blessed in so many ways, and I am beyond grateful for this beautiful life. XOXO

Forever,

Ellie 🖤

OTHER TITLES BY ELLIE WADE

The Flawed Heart Series
Finding London
Keeping London
Loving London
Eternally London
Taming Georgia

The Choices Series
A Beautiful Kind of Love
A Forever Kind of Love
A Grateful Kind of Love

The Beautiful Souls Collection
Bared Souls
Kindred Souls
Captivated Souls
Fated Souls
Destined Souls

The Heroes of Fire Station Twelve
Fragment

Found

Stand-alones

Chasing Memories

Forever Baby

A Hundred Ways to Love

ABOUT THE AUTHOR

Ellie Wade resides in southeast Michigan with her husband, three children, and three dogs. She has a master's in education from Eastern Michigan University, and she is a huge University of Michigan sports fan. She loves the beauty of her home state, especially the lakes and the gorgeous autumn weather. When she is not writing, she is reading, snuggling up with her kids, or spending time with family and friends. She loves traveling and exploring new places with her family.

Made in the USA
Columbia, SC
16 March 2024